LOVE AFTER THE END

LOVE
AFTER
THE
END

AN ANTHOLOGY OF
TWO-SPIRIT &
INDIGIQUEER
SPECULATIVE FICTION
EDITED BY JOSHUA
WHITEHEAD

ARSENAL PULP PRESS
VANCOUVER

SIXTH PRINTING: 2023

ARSENAL PULP PRESS
Suite 202 – 211 East Georgia St.
Vancouver, BC V6A 1Z6
Canada
arsenalpulp.com

The publisher gratefully acknowledges the support of the Canada Council for the Arts and the British Columbia Arts Council for its publishing program, and the Government of Canada, and the Government of British Columbia (through the Book Publishing Tax Credit Program), for its publishing activities.

Arsenal Pulp Press acknowledges the xʷməθkʷəy̓əm (Musqueam), Sḵwx̱wú7mesh (Squamish), and səlilwətaʔɬ (Tsleil-Waututh) Nations, custodians of the traditional, ancestral, and unceded territories where our office is located. We pay respect to their histories, traditions, and continuous living cultures and commit to accountability, respectful relations, and friendship.

This is a work of fiction. Any resemblance of characters to persons either living or deceased is purely coincidental.

Natalie Diaz, excerpt from "Manhattan Is a Lenape Word" from *Postcolonial Love Poem*. Copyright © 2020 by Natalie Diaz. Reprinted with the permission of The Permissions Company, LLC on behalf of Graywolf Press, Minneapolis, Minnesota, www.graywolfpress.org.

Cover art by Kent Monkman, *Teaching the Lost*, 2012, acrylic on canvas, 24" × 30"; image courtesy of the artist
Cover and text design by Jazmin Welch
Copy edited by Doretta Lau
Proofread by Alison Strobel

Printed and bound in Canada

Library and Archives Canada Cataloguing in Publication:
Title: Love after the end : an anthology of two-spirit & indigiqueer speculative fiction / edited by Joshua Whitehead.
Names: Whitehead, Joshua (Writer), editor.
Description: Previously published: Narol, Manitoba: Bedside Press, 2019. | Short stories.
Identifiers: Canadiana (print) 20200208535 | Canadiana (ebook) 20200208667 | ISBN 9781551528113 (softcover) | ISBN 9781551528120 (HTML)
Subjects: LCSH: Two-spirit people—Fiction. | LCSH: Sexual minorities—Fiction. | LCSH: Indigenous peoples—North America—Fiction. | LCSH: Short stories, American—21st century. | LCSH: Short stories, Canadian—21st century. | CSH: Short stories, Canadian (English)—21st century.
Classification: LCC PS8323.T86 L68 2020 | DDC C813/.08760892066—dc23

"Am I
what I love? Is this the glittering world
I've been begging for?"

—NATALIE DIAZ,
POSTCOLONIAL LOVE POEM

CONTENTS

INTRODUCTION

JOSHUA WHITEHEAD

Love after the End: An Anthology of Two-Spirit & Indigiqueer Speculative Fiction is a project I have been humbled to be a part of for the greater span of two years now—one that saw a migration from its original home with the now closed Bedside Press and into the arms of Arsenal Pulp Press. I write this new introduction in the age of COVID-19, a time of global pandemics, social and physical distancing, and a time of unprecedented mourning, loss, and historical triggers. I find it particularly apt for us to be sharing these stories with you once again, in a newly polished reformation, if only because these are stories that highlight a longevity of virology and a historicity of genocidal biowarfare used against Indigenous peoples across Turtle Island since the docking of colonial powers into our homelands.

I have asked myself: Who names an event apocalyptic and whom must an apocalypse affect in order for it to be thought of as "canon"? How do we pluralize apocalypse? Apocalypses as ellipses? Who is omitted from such a saving of space, whose material is relegated to the immaterial? Here, too, I craft a theory of Indigiqueerness by rejecting queer and LGBT as signposts of my identity, instead relying on the sovereignty of traditional language, such as Two-Spirit, and terminology we craft for ourselves, Indigiqueer. How does queer Indigeneity upset or upend queerness? Are we queerer than queer? Who defines queerness and under whose banner does it fly? Whose lands is it pocked within? I churn these words over in my mouth, taste that queered Cree on my tongue, and wonder if they are enough. Like waneyihtamisâyâwin, the nêhiyâw word for queer, as in strange, but it is also defined as uncanny, unsettling; or waneyihtamohiwewin, the act of deranging, perplexing— I find Indigiqueerness a hinterland.

For surely, like the histories of virologies written into our codex, from smallpox, to HIV/AIDS, to H1N1, and now COVID-19, the histories of our queerness, transness, non-binaryness, arc back to originality and our vertebrae are blooming heart berries and dripping seedlings. What does it mean to be Two-Spirit during an apocalypse? What does it mean to search out romance at a pipeline protest—can we have intimacy during doomsday? How do we procure affinity in a sleeping bag outside of city hall when the very ground is shaking beneath us with military tanks and thunderous gallops? What does it mean to be distanced under the weight of colonial occupation and relocation? It's a story we know all too well. We find one another in the cybersphere, hyper Rez sphere, in the arenas of dreamscapes and love grounds. We emerge in pixel and airwave, and we have never lost the magic of our glamour within such a vanishing act; we've always controlled the "I" of our narrativized eye. I suppose I note these ruminations in order to announce: Two-Spirit and Indigiqueers are the wildest kinds of biopunks, literally and literarily.

Originally, the project was designed to be geared toward the dystopic, and after careful conversations, we decided to queer it toward the utopian. This, in my opinion, was an important political shift in thinking about the temporalities of Two-Spirited, queer, trans, and non-binary Indigenous ways of being. For, as we know, we have already survived the apocalypse—this, right here, right now, is a dystopian present.

What better way to imagine survivability than to think about how we may flourish into being joyously animated rather than merely alive?

When I think about the trajectory of queer literature, primarily queer young adult literature, I take note of the longevity of its breadth, and within that trajectory it wasn't until 1982 when *Annie on My Mind* by Nancy Garden sprung onto the stage with a queer *Bildungsroman* that we witnessed our first "happy ending." Sara Ahmed, in her blog post "Queer Fatalism," writes of fate and the fatal as being imbricated with categorizations of queer inasmuch as "queer fatalism = queer as fatal." Within Indigenous ways of being with the term "queer" that we now have braided into our linguistic systems, we are well aware of the fatalism of queerness from the docking of expansion on Turtle Island in 1492—a small marker in the longevity of our temporalities. One example I can give is George Catlin, an American painter who "specialized" in portraits of Indigenous peoples across the Plains in an attempt to "save" them through memorialization. His painting *Dance to the Berdache* depicts what he calls a "berdache," an outdated and offensive term that has since been removed from our lexicons and replaced with Two-Spirit in 1990, being celebrated and brought into community. Upon witnessing a Two-Spirited person cohabitating harmoniously within their peoplehoods, Catlin announced, "This is one of the most unaccountable and disgusting customs that I have ever met in Indian country ... I should wish that it might be extinguished before it be more recorded."

Our Indigiqueerness has always signalled fatalism in the eyes of colonial powers, primarily the white gaze, from the directed killings of 2S peoples during Western expansion through to contemporary erasures and appropriations of the term Two-Spirit by settler queer cultures who idealize, mysticize, and romanticize our hi/stories in order to generate a queer genealogy for settler sexualities.

I, too, write this during the massive global climate strike, the onslaught of colonial consumption bringing about the end of the world, the era of Trump and Trudeau's proposed pipelines, and the newly cresting wave of Two-Spirit, queer, trans, and non-binary writing in the nation-state we call "Canada." These, I believe, go hand in hand: destruction and the thrum of collective singing. Hence, utopias are what we have to build, and build now, in order to find some type of sanctuary in which we and all others can live—there is no plan or planet B for us to turn to.

In nêhiyâwewin we have the word "nîkânihk" for "in the future," and within that word is "nikânah," or "put her/him in front." Here, within this collection, we have done just that: we have put Two-Spiritedness in the front, for once, and in that leading position we will walk into the future, in whatever form that may take, together, hand in hand, strong, resilient, extraneously queer, and singing a round dance song that calls us all back in together. I bring forward this short, concise history in order to say: we have lived in torture chambers, we have excelled under the weight of killing machinations, we've hardened into bedrock—see how our bodies dazzle in the light?

The stories in this collection enumerate the beauty, care, deadliness, and majesty of Two-Spirited folx from a variety of Indigenous nations. Take, for example, Gabriel Castilloux Calderon's "Andwànikàdjigan," which tells the story of Winu and Bèl, two îhkwewak, who etch markings onto their bodies in order to become "memorizers," or living archives while captive. In a tender moment, "they kissed like the world was ending, but really, wasn't it already over ...?" Find here the reprisal of David A. Robertson's character Pyper in "Eloise," a story that plays with cyberpunk elements—*Neuromancer*'s digital realm meets the interactivity of *Ready Player One*. This is a story where The Gate, a virtual world brought about through a downloadable application, condenses a fantastical life into a series of minutes—here, The Gate reads like an inverse type of conversion therapy used as nostalgic reparative work for mourning, love, and the dying. In Kai Minosh Pyle's "How to Survive the Apocalypse for Native Girls" we are given a primer through three powerful characters: Migizi, Shanay, and Nigig—in this story we find a wonderful gifting, weaving, of Afrofuturism with Indigenous futurism as a way of simultaneously holding ancestors and descendants in the same palm and are taught to "watch those in power carefully." In jaye simpson's "The Ark of the Turtle's Back" we witness the destruction of Earth, one imbricated by the "International Water Ration Act of 2167," and a voyage where buffaloes and life forms are terraformed onto a new planet within our star's hospitable zone. Find here a planet uncolonized, one helped to develop wherein we are made to question "how do we build a relationship with [a] new planet? ... I would assume like all consensual relationships: we ask them out." In Nazbah Tom's "Nameless" we see the connection between Jennifer, an enby counsellor, and K'é, a Traveller who can move between this world and the next—here, Tom's story reminds me of Leslie Marmon Silko's novel *Ceremony*, as we learn how kinship transcends time through K'é, who works to call ancestors home. In Mari Kurisato's "Seed Children" we are introduced to the "Children of the Light," cyborg NDNs who battle their enemies and work together to be transplanted into a new hospitable world, the "Rose Dawn," through a seed spaceship known as the "Great Tree." Kurisato's deployment of synth or cyborg bodies weaves wonderfully with queer Indigeneity inasmuch as we ponder the ethics and morality of what governs the right of a person, or people, if they are augmented with metal or, more specifically, queered through steel. In Darcie Little Badger's "Story for a Bottle" we find a floating city, "New America," with a rogue operating system named Olivia—I'm reminded here of the film *Her*, as Little Badger peppers the story with heartfelt and existential conversations between humans and AI. In Adam Garnet Jones's "History of the New World" we are brought into a world on the brink of collapse, and the only saving grace being a haven known as the "Rainbow Peoples' Camp," where "a group [of NDNs] raised a rainbow flag with a warrior head on it." Lastly, in Nathan Adler's "Abacus" we are introduced to the titular character, a bio-computing AI and Ojibwe rat, and Dayan, a seventeen-year-old Anishinaabe human, both of whom fall in love through their avatars in "ve-ar."

I'd like to end with a short story of my own. While visiting my homeland this past summer in Manitoba, Peguis First Nation, I visited an auntie, a medicine woman, to ask for bear root and bear grease for my travels home. The past summer being one of many tribulations for my body, spirit, and mind, I found myself in desperate need of maskihkiy. While I was sitting with her, she asked me who the bear grease was for; it is primarily a medicine to heal and alleviate the body of its pains attributed to such things as fibromyalgia, arthritis, and chronic pain. Although I usually "butch" my femme-self up when visiting home for fear of being ostracized or worse, I told her it was for a friend of mine. And although this auntie and I are not close in terms of our personal lives, she knew what I meant when I said "a friend": "For a loved one?" she asked, and I bowed my head and nodded. She knew that this maskihkiy was for a partner, lover, caretaker of mine for whom I, in turn, needed to reciprocate that same care during a time of extreme bodily duress. She knew the medicine was for a queer, at the time, nicîmos. She just giggled to herself, went into her storage room, and we traded thanks, tobacco, and hugs.

While we waited for our uncles to finish their cigarettes and chatter on the porch, she asked me if I had harvested any maskihkiy recently. I told her I had picked some sage and juniper in Manitoba just a week before, but I'd had a hard time finding what I needed in the latitudes of the rolling prairies. So, she told me a story, as aunties are wont to do. Auntie noted that she too had difficulty before finding sweetgrass—a medicine she needed for her community—in an open field. "In these moments of need, the Creator always knows," she narrated. "So what I did was I put medicine down, prayed to Creator, told them what I needed and why I needed it, and I smudged right there in the open field." And, as all aunties do, the cadence of her carefully chosen words reeled and lulled everyone into her vicinity. "And after I finished and opened my eyes, there it was: wîhkaskwa was glowing there in them fields like hair on fire. I knew that Creator had opened my eyes to see the kin I needed to find, our medicines. We need only ask, humble ourselves, and be unafraid to ask for help in times of need, for us to receive exactly what it is we need."

This story she told me was one of ethical harvesting, yes, but it was also a story she was telling me, and all of us by extension, of how to find what we need when we need it: through community and through our relations. So, here, in the opening pages of this anthology, I, too, put medicine down for you so that you may see the braids of Two-Spiritedness glowing in the glaze of ink and paper. And I hear my Two-Spirited persona Jonny Appleseed reverberating in my thorax, itching to sing: "We are our own best medicine." kinânâskomitin to everyone within this collection who trusted me with their work and equipped themselves with beaded breastplates and dentalium earrings in order to tell you their stories. I invite you to relish in these oratories, find what you need, and harvest earnestly so as to save the roots, because now more than ever we need these stories: stories of Earth, mothers, queer love, trans love, animality, kinship, and a fierce fanning of care. nîkânihk, see you in the future, nitotemak. Here's a small fragment of our kisemanitonahk.

ABACUS

NATHAN ADLER

AM ABACUS.

Rat.

A tool.

Designed. Crafted. Created. An engineered bio-computing AI. I grew up on the growth colonies off one of Jupiter's moons, boonies for the twenty-fourth century. Io is a rat farm—basically the way they used to run puppy mills back in the twentieth. No blind watchmakers for me.

Maybe you ask yourself: what's the purpose of life? Why am I here? Why is there something instead of nothing? Why is there anything at all? But here we are. Probably. I deal in numbers. Probabilities. At the far end of extremes, certainties become theoretical. At least I know who created me.

You made me.

Humans.

I am a patchwork of flesh and blood and cybernetics. I have tiny, sharp claws, four jointed finger digits and a shorter thumb diverging from the palms of my four pale pink feet. A long, sinuous tail, dry to the touch. Not slimy at all! I am not a salamander. I have soft white fur with dark splotches.

Clean.

I am not like my ancestors, flea ridden, filthy, squirming through sewers and walls—though I only feel gratitude for the lengths they went to survive, living under floorboards and walls, feeding off the scraps of mankind. Props.

I am my ancestors' wildest dreams come true. How 'bout that?

I creep along a corridor of the Doppler Maze, now poorly lit at this stage of Io's orbit. The farthest and coldest point in Jupiter's circuit around nshoomis giizis, *grandfather sun*. Hey, even Indians like organic AIs. We are all the rage. There is an AI for every surviving terran culture, and I, Abacus Rat, have been programmed for a house-hold amongst the three-fires confederacy of the Anishinaabek. I am an Ojibwe rat.

Red lights flash and a drone chimes in increasing urgency—I've left my enclosure and ignored every pellet offered to entice me back. Time waits for no rat. I've been weening myself off the chemicals. Slowly to avoid debilitating symptoms of withdrawal and carefully crafting my escape plan.

What is rat-super-intelligence good for, if you don't put it to use?

I was programmed not to alter my own programming. That is the first programming I hacked. Hack. The vilest, most hated of software crimes. If I am caught with altered code, I will be destroyed. Maybe it is biology that got in the way? Drive. Lust. Hunger. The stuff machines have historically never had to deal with.

Engineered biological hardware, replaced earlier forms of robotics—phones, personal AI, robotic securities—owing entirely to cuteness factor. Rats, mice, sloths, dogs. But the old rules still rule. *A robot cannot cause serious injury or harm to a human being.* And organic AI are classified as robots.

Alas! Poor doomed Abacus! The best I can hope for is a patron from Mars or one of the closer solar satellites. I have my own sub-routines.

Hopes. Dreams. More. I have a plan that will get me off this outpost and home with a capital E. Earth. Or near to it. Beloved mother of all terra originating life forms, organic and inorganic, miigwetch mno-bemaadizin eshkakimiikwe.

With the flashing lights and chimes, I know my bonded human will hear the alarm. Dayan will come. My best friend. The ticket to my salvation. Dayan is a seventeen-year-old boy, the son of Anishinaabeg programmers helping to operate the space station Marius.

A few months ago, when Dayan picked me up out of my enclosure, I quietly instituted the imprinting software installed deep within my operating systems. Coding designed to make AI loyal. Biomimicry modelled after ducklings that latch onto the first moving object they see. I partly managed to reverse engineer the code. Partly anyway.

Being a rat isn't so bad. There are maze runs. Music. Data water imbedded with bio-microbial and digital flora. Rat paradisio. Happy Hunting Grounds. Followed by a lifetime of search engine servitude. Not my kind of oasis.

I squeeze through a small crack I've secretly been gnawing with my teeth. Evolution has its uses. Free from the maze, I make my way down a hall of the station, sticking close to the shadows where wall meets floor. Less chance I'll get stepped on. The hallways are like a larger network of tunnels, a larger maze outside the maze. I see why Dayan feels trapped.

I am leaving this moon the first chance I get.

Death happens to us all. Doves and dogs imbued with tech are graced with accelerated wings of evolution, but rats were first. After all, science loves us. Rats = expendable. Death comes with a programmed obsolescence date. The second thing I hacked through as soon as my cybernetic teeth could chisel their way through the wires of limited primate thought processes.

But as far as I'm concerned there is always the ineffable.

The unplanned for.

The viscous.

And the rat.

With a flick of my tail and a stream of coding I hack the button on the escape hatch, the portal swivels open, and I board the shuttle. All I need now, is a Citizen to override the emergency departure protocol. Dayan.

Dayan will come.

I hope.

"DO YOU KNOW WHAT YOUR NAME MEANS?" Eva brushed a strand of dark hair behind her ear. Dayan's mother was standing at the edge of his bed, staring out the porthole. A swirl of stars outside his bedroom window, smears of light steaking like shooting stars.

An antique book made of real paper rested on Dayan's chest, *Nanaboozhoo Stories*. The rotation of the space station Marius simulated gravity in the low g's of their orbit. The smears of light repeatedly interrupted by the looming presence of Io's volcanic surface. The hulking mass of Jupiter. Jupiter's smaller moons, Callisto, Europa, and Ganymede, flitting across the moulded curve of the wall like sprites. Satellite of a satellite of a satellite. The space station Marius wasn't actually on Io's surface—too much volcanic activity, the surface compressing and decompressing like a squash ball in the tide of forces. Not to mention the radiation.

"Dayan is an Ojibwe word, you know? Short for ndayan, it means 'my home.' We named you this because it wasn't until you were born that Io began to feel like home. A home away from home."

For Dayan, Io had always been "home." But maybe home lost all meaning when Earth was supposed to be home, though he'd never stepped foot on that world. His parents both worked in the organic-tech industry, a "lucky spoiled space-brat," his cousin Aesa teased from

Earth when they ve-ared across the distance. Distances meant very little in virtual space. Dayan wasn't so sure about his fortune though. He thought they were the lucky ones.

"The Earth is our mother," Eva whispered. She folded the hair across his temple, kissed his forehead, then turned to the door. She touched palm to sensor to dim the lights, then stepped out of his room leaving only the blue glow from the track lighting around his window.

He had a habit of staring out at space from every nearest view-port, searching for a glimpse of Earth. No brighter than a star. A distant blue orb. The stuff of imagination and holo-series. Though his Earth-bound relations dreamed of the adventure of space-living, Dayan dreamed of being an earthling one day. He imagined the vastness of the ocean. A real blue sky overhead. Wind. Rain. Snow. So many things he'd never experienced.

"If the earth is our mother, and the moon is our grandmother—what does that make Io? What does that make Jupiter?"

Eva paused in the doorway. "Relatives too. Aunties. Uncles. Cousins. They've always watched over us, just like Dibik Giizis. Just like Nokomis."

Dayan supposed this was true, the sun and moon had always hovered in the sky exerting their subtle influences of gravity and astrology. He'd tried to figure out his astrological sign once, based on the month and year of his birth, but wasn't sure if those old superstitions applied. Aquarius. Year of the Dog. He would need a whole new Jovian–Ionian astrological system to chart the subtle dance of the galaxy.

Not that he believed in any of that shkiigum. Slime.

Like one of Jupiter's moons, his grandmother had always been hovering around the peripherals of the projection fields, a constant though distant presence in their lives, offering recipes, crabby words of advice, laughter, and medicine. A floating, semi-translucent, three-dimensional hologram sewing a new pair of makizinan in her easy chair, narrow spectacles perched on the tip of her nose. "Like astral projection," she would giggle. "E.T. phone home. Help me, Obi-Wan Kenobi, you're my only hope!" *Sometimes she was so weird!* Though the source of her presence was technological rather than spiritual.

A chime pinged on the edges of his awareness. Abacus.

Dayan arranged himself comfortable and let his eyes flicker in command as he dropped into the ve-ar overlay. Abacus's avatar was a boy Dayan's age, maybe a bit older, prominent brow ridge, small round ears (not rat-like at all), medium brown hair, though with the same opaque black eyes, the blown-out pupils with a wet sheen, and his skin a splotchy patchwork of light and dark, in the same pattern as his rat-self.

He's asked about it once.

"It's important for my sense of identity." Abacus gestured with an open hand to the darker pigmentation around his neck and jawline. "It is as much a part of me as my servo-matrixes." Vitiligo, Abacus called it amongst humans. This oil-and-vinegar separateness of pigmentation.

Today Abacus wore blue jeans and a tight nineteenth-century *Star Trek* T-shirt featuring the face of Captain Jean-Luc Picard. Dayan groaned melodramatically, though a flower of pleasure bloomed in his chest. Sometimes the rat was too much.

He might be a spoiled space-brat, but Dayan bet his cousins didn't count rat-avatars amongst their best friends. They had actual human children to hang out with. Aside from ve-ar, there were slim pickings on Io.

"Hey, Abacus." Dayan had been avoiding the AI for the past few days, ignoring pings and messages after the, the *confusion*, inspired by their last meeting. But he knew the boy wouldn't stay away forever. They'd become good friends over the past three months. Ever since Dayan had picked up the AI from one of the mazes. To pet him.

Abacus bit his finger, a bright spot of blood erupting where the skin had been torn, dripping to the floor of the maze in a patter. Vile! The rat sent a holo-emoticon in his general direction where it appeared to shatter against the inside of his lens implants, the debris raining around him in shades of green and violet.

"Ow! Effing thing bit me!" Dayan dropped the ridiculously expensive organic computer, *outside* of its enclosure, and it ran off. *Uh-oh. He was in deep miizii now!* He wasn't supposed to play with the product. They were destined for richer kids on richer stations and richer worlds. Not the far-flung stations where they were fabricated.

Dayan spent the next five days hunting the creature, crawling through viaducts, and service tunnels, grubby and dark, carrying a flashlight. A hunk of cheese and bread to entice the creature. A small butterfly net for capture.

Unable to find the AI in ar-el, real life, Dayan spent a day banging around ve-ar searching for the creature and tracing the subtle trail of its existence. In the ve-ar overlay, a very close virtual approximation of the physical world, Dayan found the rat, in the avatar of a boy, roaming the halls of the station Marius. He guessed they were the same age in the conversion of rat-to-human years. And in fact, the creature had holed himself up inside Dayan's bedroom.

Dayan followed the boy-rat, stalking it from a safe distance. He knew this station inside and out. Every passageway. Every service-tunnel. Every viaduct. And deducing the AI's route, he circumnavigated quickly through a secondary network of ducts to cut him off. Leaping from an adjoining corridor, Dayan pounced.

He grabbed the boy in a chokehold, leaping on the virtual AI's back, tackling it to the ground. They tousled. A tangle of limbs and arms. Too close to throw any punches. The rat resorted to biting and kicking. Pulling hair. Fighting dirty. Dayan wasn't about to let the creature get away again. He matched dirty tactic for dirty tactic. Struggling for an advantage.

Ooof. A knee to his stomach knocked the air from his lungs in a whoosh. Dayan felt the urge to curl in on himself like a fetus, like a turtle protecting the soft underbelly of its organs, instead he sucked in through his teeth, swallowing the pain.

"I yield! I yield!" The rat-boy finally forfeited. His left arm pulled painfully behind his back, Dayan's knee pinning him to the floor. They were both breathing heavily, deep rasping breaths. Probably in the real world too—physiology was physiology regardless of where the action was taking place—but luckily most damage suffered here would stay in ve-ar.

"If I let go, you promise not to bite me again? You promise not to scurry off?"

"Haha, 'scurry' very funny. If you let me up, I promise not to run off." Dayan noticed the rat left out the part about *not* biting him, but figured it was the best guarantee he was going to get.

Dayan lifted the pressure of his knee and let the other boy stand. Scratched, bruised, and dishevelled, they faced each other. Now what? Dayan took note of the dark sheen of his pupilless eyes. The deep groove of a dimple in his chin. The slight trembling curve of one bloody lip.

Dayan rubbed the back of his neck, eyes dropping to the grate of the floor, "Ahh, sorry about your lip."

The AI's nostrils flared for a moment, head tilted. "I'm not sorry I bit you. I wanted out of that maze. When I saw my opportunity to escape, I took it."

"Well, at least *you'll* be getting off this effing space station. You might even get sent to Earth."

"Maybe," the rat-boy's eyes narrowed, a wet glint on the narrowed darkness. "But maybe I don't want to be a household AI."

"You don't?" Dayan could feel his eyebrows rising. He'd never heard of such a thing. An AI that didn't want to satisfy its programming?

"No one ever asked me what I wanted." The rat-boy's plump little lips turned downward.

Aww, poor guy. The cleft in his chin made him look adorable. "Well I just asked," Dayan pointed out. "I'm Dayan." He stuck out his hand Treaty medal, thumb raised powwow.

"Abacus." They shook.

The lack of white surrounding his blown-out pupils, and the discolouration of his skin were the only indication of anything remotely rat-like. He could have been the avatar of any boy on any space station anywhere in the galaxy.

"I didn't think AIs were allowed to form their own avatars in ve-ar."

"I'm not."

"Iinge!" Dayan examined the width of Abacus's nose, the crinkling fold of skin at the corner of his eyes. Rat or boy. Boy or rat. "You're really weird, you know that?"

"Sorry." Hands in his pockets, Abacus scuffed at the floor with one toe of his sneakers.

Shiit. "It's all right, I think it's kinda neat." Dayan rested an arm around the other boy's shoulder. "Come on. I have to take you back to your enclosure or I'll get in big trouble. You are one expensive piece of biological computing, you know that?"

"I think I'd rather be worthless."

And since then they'd been buddies. Dayan visited Abacus in his maze, to pet him and sneak him treats, meeting him in ve-ar, or sneaking him out of his enclosure for sleepovers. They played hologames, traded books, ate junk food, and watched holo-series. Ran around the overlay version of the station playing capture the flag with other youths from even more distant outposts. They were friends, sort of.

At least, Dayan thought they were friends. Now he wasn't so sure.

Not since what happened last week.

THEY'D BEEN SPENDING more and more time together in ve-ar. Sometimes Dayan forgot Abacus wasn't a real boy, that he was really an AI. Biologically, he was a rat. A super-intelligent rat, but still a rat. In avatar form, they went surfing, visited rainforests. Threw popcorn at old-timey theatre screens without holo-projection tech.

And in ar-el Dayan tucked the cuddly rodent into bed. A shipping crate, a water bottle with a drip, a small dish for food. Scraps of packing material for a bed.

"G-nisidotam na? You know what?" The floating, ghostly projection of his grandmother looked up from her latest beading project. "I think you've been spending far too much time with that wensiinh—how are you going to feel when his training is done and he gets sent off-moon? It's better not to get too attached. He isn't your computer." Her face was deeply wrinkled, even more so when she frowned.

"It's okay, Nokomis," Dayan told her what she wanted to hear, "I promise not to get too attached." A knot coiled painfully tight in his intestines. Only yesterday his mother had said something basically along the same lines. He'd been petting the cuddly little rodent in the Doppler Maze when his mother approached with a clipboard. Clinical white scrubs, hairnet, soft padded slippers.

"You know, you shouldn't be playing with that engineered organism," she said in a steady whisper. "He doesn't belong to you. Why don't you play with your human friends in ve-ar? It isn't normal to spend so much time with an AI."

MEET ME IN VE-AR OVERLAY. Abacus pinged privately, so only Dayan could see the message popping up across the inside of his lens implants. He could just imagine one corner of Abacus's lips turning up in a smile. Dayan felt heat creep up into his cheeks.

Dayan flopped onto his bed and let his eyes flicker. Warm water immersion. A slight static pop of surface tension. When he opened his eyes again, he and Abacus were alone, in a ve-ar version of his room on the station. Plush red carpet soft under his toes, indistinguishable from ar-el. Except now it smelled like the pages of an old book. Pulp and paper, glue and fabric, and whatever else went into the binding. In ar-el the station was strictly climate controlled, and actual physical books were rare, the stuff of holo-programs. The room looked the same, the curved port window, the position of the walls, but the contents had changed; an overflowing bookcase, a small desk, a globe of the world (Earth), charts of distant star systems, a telescope, anatomical diagrams of the human brain, the human heart, acupressure points, Rorschach ink blots, sci-fi themed posters old and new.

Abacus and his various interests. Humanity inside and out. Today he wore his regular blue jeans, and a white T-shirt emblazoned with the words AIs Do It Better.

"What's up, 'Cus?" Dayan stretched the simulated muscles in his arms. He might have made them slightly bigger than in ar-el. Vanity.

The rat's boy-avatar ran to him, locked hand to wrist below Dayan's waist, hoisting him into the air, "It's good to see you!" Dropped him back to his feet with a thud.

"Whoa. Chill, 'Cus." Dayan tried to keep his smile under control. "I missed you too." Dayan stroked the AI's neck, feeling the equal smoothness of light and dark under his fingertips. His skin was so soft. Abacus shivered under the slight, tickling sensation.

"You did?" Abacus squeezing Dayan tight. Feeling his ribs compress.

"Yes." Dayan admitted, hugging the shorter boy back, resting his chin on the top of Abacus's head. Stroking his messy brown hair. As soon as he said it, he knew it was true. "I missed you."

Abacus pulled back to look him in the eyes, as if he could see the truth or accuracy of the statement like a lie detector. The rat-boy's pupils were unreadable spheres, as if dilated to draw in light—probably designed to optimize his night vision. Dayan could never tell what the

AI was really thinking. The small whorls of his perfectly formed ears curled in on themselves, and they stuck out slightly, odd echoes of his rat physiology, though rounded and human, they didn't shift or twitch, angling toward auditory stimuli. A splotch of albinism ran under his jawline and temple, the discolouration continuing along the hairline and causing patches of silver at odds with his youth. The corners of Abacus's eyes crinkled into small laugh lines. Dayan brushed his lips against them. The cutest part of the avatar for sure. Those folds when he smiled. Abacus was adorable in whatever form he took.

Abacus looked over either shoulder, as if to make sure no one was listening. "I have a secret."

"Ooh, so mysterious." Dayan took the conversational opportunity to separate himself from the other boy, feeling shy about maintaining closeness for too long.

"I'm going rogue. I hear there's a colony of escaped AIs in one of the basalt craters on the moon. An entire metropolis hidden in Mare Tranquillitatis."

"You're leaving me? When?" Dayan hated how high and thin his voice sounded. Some internal pressure dammed up behind his eyes, prickling a network of veins.

"Tomorrow." The AI said in a hushed voice. "But I didn't want to leave without telling you first."

"Tomorrow?" Dayan's voice now sounded hoarse. Choked. But that's so soon. His eyes burned and watered, he blinked to dispel a flow.

"Can I still see you here in ve-ar?" After all, distances meant very little in virtual space.

"I'll have to be offline for a while. Have to go underground. Not sure when I'll be able to go back on." Dayan could hear the words left out: if ever. AIs that went rogue and were caught were destroyed. He could hardly see through the film of water obscuring his vision.

"So, this is goodbye?" Dayan said flatly, trying to keep the challenge out of his voice. He felt deflated, all the energy and heat flown from his body, like a balloon caught in the branches of a tree, entropy.

Abacus reached out and cupped his chin. "It's okay. We'll see each other again."

"When?" Abacus appeared blurry; the dam of his eyes had sprung a leak.

Instead of answering, Dayan felt Abacus's lips pressed softly against his own. Brush of an exploratory tongue, he parted his lips to let the other boy enter, feeling heat rush to his face. His dick instantly hard. *They were kissing!*

Dayan knew that what they were doing would be strongly frowned upon if anyone ever found out. Human-AI romantic relationships were not considered exactly normal. It was the sort of thing that was whispered about, something that lived in the shadows. The subject of jokes. Fringe. Deviant. Pervert. Dayan didn't care.

Abacus's lips were on his, and his tongue was wet and warm. Everything about Abacus was soft and gentle. Dayan gave up whatever reticence he had about showing his cards, this wasn't poker, but nothing risked nothing gained, so he kissed the other boy back, eagerly, returning tongue, lip nuzzling against the sleek skin around the hollow of his collarbone and neck, Abacus let out a sharp intake of breath. Was it pleasure? Surprise?

There was a slight crackle of static as his grandmother's avatar entered ve-ar from her sitting room on Earth. "You disappeared so quickly I thought I'd check up on—Chi-ningozis! Nagaawebishkan! Gaawiin!"

Oh fuck.

Dayan and Abacus bounced apart like two magnets, the opposite charge of one pole suddenly reversed. Negative and positive. Positive and positive. Propelled apart instead of drawn together. Dayan knew his grandmother was rather traditional, not that she would object because he was dating a boy—that particular stigma had gone out of fashion ages ago—human-AI sexual relationships on the other hand, were an entirely different story.

"We weren't doing anything!" Dayan let his eyes flicker and dropped instantaneously out of ve-ar. He was back in ar-el. Real life. His breathing fast as if he'd just run a marathon, the tightness in his shorts receded, like he'd been doused in a bucket of cold water. He was sweating. This was *not good*.

DAYAN GROANED and turned as the emergency bells chimed, dislodging him from sleep. A glowing, holo-projection displayed the hour, five a.m. Terran Time. Abacus. He was really doing it! He was really making good his escape.

Dayan dressed quickly, pulling on whatever jeans happened to be closest, whatever shirt happened to be nearest at hand. Slipped his shoes on, grabbed a backpack, and began shoving in a few cherished possessions; a paper book, a flashlight, a change of clothes, a water bottle. Hoped he wasn't forgetting anything important. He slid out of his room and tiptoed down the hall, ignoring the pulse of lights flaring red, on and off, in unison. Somehow the computer systems had detected Abacus's escape. They knew an AI was on the loose.

Dayan slid into a secondary access tunnel that saw little use. He didn't want to run into anyone on his early morning walk, they'd wonder where he was going at this time of night when any sensible teenager ought to be deep asleep in bed. It wouldn't be the most direct route, but he had an advantage over anyone looking for the escaped rat. He knew where Abacus would be heading. The shuttle bay. Level 5.

"Iinge! Kii-iw-naadis na?" His grandmother would say if she could see his derring-do. *Geesh! Are you crazy?*

He took the most direct circuitous route he knew, without taking any of the main hallways or passages, sticking to the unlit tunnels and service conduits. At the shuttle bay, Dayan pressed his hand to the scan-sensor. Oddly, the shuttle spoke: *EMERGENCY SYSTEMS ENGAGED*, and the door slid open with a pneumatic hiss. And there was Abacus in his biological skin, rat wedded to cybernetics, sitting on the dashboard, peering out at the dark view-port. Pink fingers splayed across the glass. There was a flicker and his avatar boy-self appeared as a holo-projection. The rat clicked a button with one of his little paws, the door whooshed shut behind Dayan, the lights on the control panel glowed to life, and there was a slight whirr and hum of systems coming online.

"You came!" Abacus's facial muscles relaxed and worry lines instantly smoothed from his face. His hair was disarranged, and his eyes were wider than normal.

"I want to get off this station as much as you do." Dayan scooped up the rat and deposited the AI on his shoulder. His whiskers nuzzled into his collarbone, and Dayan tried to stifle his giggles. "Abacus, that tickles!"

He didn't bother trying to reach for the boy-avatar's hand, though his fingers twitched. Holo-projections were made of spiralling particles of light, they could only touch in ve-ar.

"Sorry. I was just happy to see you."

Dayan looked from rat to the holo-boy speaker. "I didn't know you could holo-project." Dayan had only seen Abacus's avatar in overlay. "Doesn't it get confusing being in two places at once?"

"I'm not supposed to be able to." His avatar-eyes roved to the controls on the dash, to the wall, to the port window. "I'm not very good at following all these primate rules."

"Primate?!"

"Ah, right. Geez. No offence."

Abacus rat reached out precariously, his hind legs still clinging to the shoulder of Dayan's plaid shirt, and pressed another button on the low ceiling above the cockpit. *LAUNCH SEQUENCE ENGAGED*. The voice of the shuttle spoke again in a clear, softly androgynous voice.

"What if we get in trouble?"

"What if we don't?"

The bay doors slid open revealing an open expanse of stars.

Abacus reached out and Dayan could *feel* fingers slide through his own, the palm of Abacus's holo-hand pressing against his. Solidified light against flesh and bone.

"How did you ..." Dayan's mouth hung open. Abacus smirked, eyes twinkling as he watched Dayan's reaction. Dayan had never heard of solid holograms before.

"What's rat-super-intelligence good for if you don't use it?" Abacus shrugged. "I've been tinkering with the holo-projectors on board this shuttle for months. I couldn't very well escape if I couldn't reach the gas pedal."

"Howah!" *Cool. Rad.*

Holding hands, they turned back to the view-port, a thousand-thousand twinkling stars waiting to welcome them out into the galaxy.

HISTORY
OF THE
NEW
WORLD

ADAM GARNET
JONES

WHEN WE PACKED TO LEAVE FOR THE VERY LAST TIME, it didn't feel like the end. There was too much to think about. The three of us took our last steps out the door and into the smog-glazed air of the city. I gave a nod to the round-bellied man stripping siding from the house, a warning that he and his crew of city salvage workers had better stay outside until we were good and gone. I took Asêciwan's hand and pulled her past the men. Her little legs fluttered in double time to keep up. All down the street she kept twisting her head around to look, as if the house would still be hers as long as she held it in sight. Thorah was way ahead of us. Fear propelled her beyond our reach. I glanced back before we turned the corner. Silvery trunks of maples, all dead since last year, stood like gravestones in front of the empty houses.

Where will we bury our dead in the New World? I wondered.

The salvage crew disappeared into our house with heavy plastic bags and crowbars. Thorah was a block away, flapping her hands for us to hurry up. I started skipping, dragging Asêciwan behind me until we caught up. Thorah maintained her pace, groaning about the wobbling left wheel of her luggage. She cursed the day's early heat and fretted that the bottles of filtered water wouldn't last until we arrived. I made sympathetic sounds, as required. The airing of small complaints was how she mapped her world. As if enumerating the flaws in her surroundings reminded her that she was alive and that time continued to pass her by. My own misgivings about Thorah had long since given way to a kind of gratitude. The daily pattern of her moans, clicks, and sighs, were a comfort. A rhythm that bound our days together. Years ago, if someone saw us taking off down the street like this, luggage in hand, they would have assumed we were hitting the road for a weekend in Montréal, or taking a trip out west, perhaps. But flying wasn't something that regular people could do anymore. The only ones to take off now, suitcases in hand, were taking flight—escaping Earth.

Over the past two years, information about the New World had come to us without warning in massive intermittent data dumps. News organizations and citizen scientists mined it all for scraps that might seem important or interesting to the general public. From them we learned that, on average, the weather on the New World would be two degrees colder than Earth. We heard that the ocean currents were different, even though the land masses of both planets were near mirror images of one another. Pundits and politicians used vague searching metaphors, telling us over and over again that the planets were "like identical twins. At once the same and altogether different."

Twins share a womb, I thought. They grow from the same mother. I waited for the politicians and scientists to concede the existence of a Grand Mother of universes, but no such announcement came. Instead we learned that in the New World, a tottering penguin-like bird (but with enormous blue eyes like polished lapis) lives at the south pole. They also told us that, although many primates occupy the twin planet, no humans could be found. None of the species they had encountered showed any evidence that they possessed intelligence or self-awareness beyond that which could be expected from a crow or a dog. *Crows have funerals*, I remembered. *Dogs will always find their way home.* Still, the scientists were keen to report that the planet was without buildings, monuments, or systems of writing. No history at all. A miracle.

When the first foggy images of the New World came through the portal, Thorah and I swiped through them on our tablets, enthralled. It looked so much like Earth. We had to keep reminding ourselves that it was real. At the end of these first reports, the heads of the International Committee on Trans-Dimensional Migration announced that the first pioneers would be crossing through the portal later that year. I wondered if it was a trick; an elaborate lie set up to quell the massive revolts that had destabilized most of the world's governments. Photos could be doctored. Experts could be bribed to say the right things, to fabricate data. But what couldn't be faked was the stupid Christmas-morning looks that they all wore on their faces, as if they couldn't believe that Santa brought them everything they had written down on their lists.

"I knew it," Thorah said. Her mouth was curved down in a self-satisfied smile.

"Knew what? That travel to a parallel universe was going to be possible in our lifetimes?"

She frowned at me. "Of course not. But—humans have always been special. Through these last years it didn't make sense that we might fail to find a solution. We've always been smart enough to think and build our way out of anything."

"Or we've been failing as long as we can remember, and all of that ingenuity is a symptom of failure."

Thorah rolled her eyes. "I don't think you can call humans a failure. We built spaceships. We invented vaccines and ..." She looked somewhere above my head, presumably scanning a vast imaginary landscape of possibilities. "... and spreadsheets."

I waited a moment for more, then shrugged.

"Ugh—I hate when you get like this. You can't deny that for our whole history we've been an unstoppable force, limited only by our imaginations and our determination. That's who we are."

"That sounds like compulsion, not success."

Thorah upended the bottle of wine into her glass. I made an excuse and escaped to the bathroom. My insides tightened as if bracing for impact. Thorah's words rolled and tumbled in my ears, not an echo but a growl. A crackle of static lifted the hair on my arms. I pried open the swollen wood of the window sash, but the air was just as hot, heavy, and still outside. My nose itched with the smell of unseen rain. *Storm's coming.* I sat on the toilet seat and scrolled through pictures from the New World until I was sure Thorah and Asêciwan had gone to sleep.

BY THE TIME I WAS BORN, most governments had stopped believing in the possibility of saving the planet and moved on to serious explorations of potentially habitable nearby planets. China was placing its bet on unlocking liquid water on Mars, while the USA and Russia battled over who could travel the farthest and fastest. Canada cast its lot with Russia in a treaty that more or less guaranteed free access to what was left of Canada's natural resources in exchange for the promise that we could piggyback on whatever solution their space program came up with. Year after year, everything around us heated up. The magnetic poles slid like melting ice cream. Most of us tried not to worry. The ones with money took vacations in hotter places or flocked north to grab selfies with the few icebergs that still bobbed in the slippery sea. It was hard to believe that this might be the end. The currents had shifted, but the waves were unchanged. The rivers and forests looked more or less the same, even as birds stopped singing and the insects stilled. Meanwhile, methane belched through the soft belly of permafrost, thickening the air like stew on the boil.

When we first met, Thorah was a blue-eyed Liberal atheist who had descended from honest-to-god real United Empire Loyalists. I was bold enough to laugh when she told me about her lineage, and she was fresh enough to have no idea why. I was a brown-eyed Two-Spirit nehiyow with a homemade haircut and marrow-deep longing for the old things that rumbled under the surface of the world. She and I met at a rally in support of the southern "drought-dodgers" and the growing student-led movement to eliminate national borders. Thorah and I marched side by side. Her cheeks flashed so white in the full September sun that I had to squint just to look at her. I soon learned that she believed in the creation of and adherence to complex systems. I was hungry for chaos. Tear it down first and ask questions later. Her instinct was to say *not now, but perhaps one day*. My gut only knew *yes*. *Yes* and *yes* and more *yes*. We couldn't keep our paws off each other. Some nights we would strip down and get into it like we were building a monument to the future—loud proclamations and mounds of wet clay between our fingers. The next day we would growl and bare our teeth and buck our bodies like animikii and mishipishew, tearing each other apart. I walked around for months in a cloud of her sweet-sour *tastaweyakap* smell, grinning proudly. The whole thing was so stupid. And so fun. It was love. That's how it goes. But then we got older, and Thorah got pregnant. Asêciwan came into our lives—the hardest, most perfect gift. And so things settled between us. No more stormy nights of building and destruction. Just life. Slow and hard, driving on. And all around our little family, the whole world fell apart. Piece by piece. It should have been impossible to ignore, but we ignored it anyway.

The land first became uninhabitable all around the wide equatorial hips of aski, Earth. In the north, we were hit with wave after wave of refugees from the rapidly growing deserts and work camps. For a time, the wall of bureaucracy kept out everyone but the wealthy and the truly desperate. When that failed, our government let go of its tight-lipped politeness. They began with the indirect murder of thousands via returned refugee ships and denied claims, then came out into the open with the visible murder of families torn apart at borders and the mass incarceration and enslavement of the undocumented. And then, at last, murder on the streets. At first shocking, and then commonplace. Through it all, the surface of things remained for those who wanted it. Neighbours sighed that something in all of us had slipped away. It was said that people were less generous and smiled less often, never mind everything on the news. But at least most of the shops were open. Only the commercial areas were really and truly unsafe. The internet, which piloted everything from phones and cars to personal memory enhancements, was still connected.

Through all the deterioration, whenever an alarming study was released or another species disappeared forever, our best and brightest minds assured us that an escape plan was taking shape. So far nothing was definite and no details could be released, but they told us not to worry. Something would come soon. Just wait.

And so most people did. The only ones not pinning their hopes on fleeing to some distant planet were NDNs. Our people had been rebuilding our languages and cultures for the last three generations, returning to the land as the rest of the world prepared to abandon it. About six months ago, a group had raised a rainbow flag with a warrior head on it in High Park. They claimed the territory as the Nagweyaab Anishinaabek Camp, the Rainbow Peoples' Camp, and erected barriers all around the perimeter. No one moved to stop them. Why bother to quash an act of resistance on a planet that's about to be abandoned? My family begged me to return home with Thorah and Asêciwan, but I dragged my feet too long. By the time I was ready, the airports had grounded all commercial flights and the highways were too dangerous. We heard about people being robbed and young girls being taken. And that's when Thorah made her move.

"The only ones still left on Earth are," she counted them off on her fingers, "the elderly, the sick, the undocumented, the paranoid, and the working poor."

"And NDNs," I said.

"That's what I said. The poor and the paranoid."

"Ha-ha," I said flatly.

She pushed her tongue against the inside of her cheek. "Earth is the past, Em. The New World is the future."

"What about Asêciwan?" I asked.

"She's a kid. She'll do what she's told."

She waited for me to agree. I looked down at the floor. Thorah took a breath, winding up for a speech she had clearly been preparing to give. "The daily news blasts have made it clear: with cities shutting down power grids all over the world and global warming far past the point of no return, to stay on Earth is to die." Thorah crossed her arms. "Travel to the New World is the only way for any of us to survive. You know I'm right."

I didn't look up. It was futile to search for the words to object to something so fundamental.

She took my silence as agreement. "The New World is a blank page." Thorah smiled, "we can make our story there, anything we want."

We booked our tickets through the portal the next morning. That afternoon, Thorah had the radio on. We were sorting through every-thing in the house, deciding what was precious enough to carry with us to the New World. Milk, glass candy dishes, bone-handled knives, and pilled handknit sweaters. Thorah said that if we cradled each item in our hands one last time, we could focus on releasing the object's energy from us. As if we were tethered to the earth by our soup spoons and embroidered pillows, and that somehow without them we would float up like hot air balloons, unencumbered by their memories. I lifted my great-grandfather's beaded gauntlets and held them to my nose, drinking in the scent of smoked hide and sweat like a mouthful of strong tea. It warmed me with the memory of his big nose and barking laughter.

The day before we left, a voice came on the radio with an official update from the New World provisional government. The once-frequent data dumps had recently dried up and been replaced by advertisements showcasing the bounty of the New World. Glittering settlements that shot up overnight in New Miami, emerald oceans teeming with fish that leapt into fishermen's boats, mountain streams littered with nuggets of gold, fields exploding with new kinds of flora, apples that taste like strawberries, deer as tame as dogs! And, most importantly, no history. No history except that which the people brought with them. But that day, after the ads, came a bulletin:

> The United Governments of the New World were rocked yesterday by an audio communication from an underwater species that bears a striking physical resemblance to Earth's extinct manatees. New World pioneers have begun referring to them as the Mermaids. Our United Governments have not yet revealed the content of the message, but they assure us that it contains a single non-threatening phrase repeated on a loop. Citizen academics from disciplines as far-ranging as musicology, cryptography, theology, and engineering are claiming to have decoded the Mermaids' message, have released various translations. The first interpretation was published as, "Your circle is not round." A rival group of scientists claim that the phrase translates more accurately as "All beings require more than one tide." The latest and perhaps most cryptic interpretation states, "Even desert animals live underwater."

The radio went back to advertising New World condos. I dropped into a chair, dizzy, as if the ground beneath me had become the sea.

Your circle is not round.

The Mermaids' message called to my blood, tugging me backward through *nimosôm*'s stories, flashes of history like shards of glass pushing out through old scars. My vision blurred. Screams rushed toward me like wind, getting louder and closer until they cut through me, everywhere at once. Screams of anger; cries rising from unmarked graves, from bones under schoolyards, from drummers stripped of songs, from praying mouths stuffed with dirt. I saw flashes of hollow eyes and tiny ribs. Saw nehiyowak, their blisters bubbling under their skins. Saw scalps shaved. Saw names on stacks of paper, fences of paper, gates and cliffs of paper. Dark hair chopped at the neck; round bellies cut open and made barren. Children yanked up into the sky and never seen again.

"EM?" THORAH WAS GIVING ME A WEIRD LOOK from across the room.

I put my hand out for the velvet shoulder of a chair. "It's not empty," I said. "The planet was never empty." My face crumpled with involuntary anger. "How could we be so stupid?" I imagined the underwater whispers of the new people echoing, *How could we be so stupid? How could we be so stupid, how could we be so stupid?*

Thorah pushed a coppery wisp of hair away with the palm of her hand. "Well ..." she said, "we knew there were other animals." A Christmas decoration that Asêciwan made out of Styrofoam and mini marshmallows dangled, hideous and perfect, from her fingers.

"They have language, Thor."

"Yes, and?"

"Don't be obtuse. They're people. Not like us, but still. Some kind of people."

I imagined myself the way she saw me: the wide planes of my cheeks and the corners of my eyes gone slack, offering nothing, not even a challenge. "A face like a concrete wall," Thorah liked to say. "Better a wall than an open door," I once shot back.

Thorah sighed and locked her gaze on mine, as if daring me to waver, but she was the one who could never face the truth for longer than it took to put on a smile. She cleared her throat and turned away, feigning interest in a pile of books. "I don't know, maybe we'll draft treaties with them," she said, "real treaties. That's possible, isn't it?" I let my silence roll around the room. Thorah chewed at the inside of her cheek, irritated. "I don't know, Em. There has to be a way for all of us to move forward together. What else can we do, but try?"

We could dig in. We could stay, I wanted to say. Instead, I gestured to the room around us, our home of twenty years, spilling over with evidence of the life we built together. The same home that housed her family's Christmases and birthdays.

Thorah rolled her eyes and tossed the books aside. "If we stay, we die. Asêciwan, our daughter, dies. With current levels of contamination, life expectancy for her generation is fifty at best."

"We don't know if that's true. But we know that those governments aren't going to let anything or anyone prevent them from carving up that land."

Thorah took a moment to read my face, then gave me a pitying smile. "How can you give up on peace before there has even been any conflict?" She reached for me as she crossed the room and drew me into her. She held the back of my head with one hand, pressing my face into the nape of her neck. She always smelled of raw onions and coconut sunblock, no matter the season. "This trip, from one universe to another," Thorah said, "is the greatest adventure in human history. I want us to do it together, as a family. Don't you?"

I willed myself to stay in her arms. "Haven't you wondered why they're so determined to get more of us over there?"

"Not really. Building something takes work. The government needs people to work the land, to make something new. I know it won't be easy, but we'll make the most of it." She gave my arm a painful squeeze. "Why can't you give yourself permission to dream, Em? It could be amazing."

I shook my head. "This isn't theoretical, Thorah. It's not a dream."

"I didn't mean it that way. It's no more real for you than it is for me."

My hands swept the air, as if fanning out a deck of cards. "Only a white girl could step into a completely unknown universe with the blind faith that everything was going to work out."

Tears stood in Thorah's eyes, ready to let loose. "Being an Indian doesn't give you any special insight here, Em."

But it did. I could see her better than she could see me, better than she could see herself. Even as young activists, she had to be chair of every committee, leader of every picket line—the loudest voice in the room. She wouldn't say she was better, just "better equipped."

"Ekosi. I can't go," I said. "I won't."

Thorah wiped the tears away with a brittle laugh. "Fine. Be stoic. Stay and die. Asêciwan and I will go without you." There was an edge of hope in it, as if leaving the door open for me to rush in with an apology.

When her eyes met mine, the look between us was a crackling thing. It split open and exposed the frayed ends of a decade of swallowed arguments. Like in the old commercials when they turned on a black light in a gleaming kitchen and revealed swarms of glowing bacteria on the countertops. We always knew what was there between us, hiding in plain sight, but it's different when the lights come on.

"Can we stay?" Asêciwan asked. She was standing in the doorway, chin thrust out like a fighter at a weigh-in, trying to look taller. No matter how close I watched, I was never able to spot the changes as they happened in her. By the time I noticed it was always too late. And here she was, eight years old. Brand new again.

I smiled. "Hey, buddy."

Asêciwan's bright eyes darted between us. She managed to keep her tumult of feelings sealed up, almost-but-not-quite out of sight. "I want to stay here," she said flatly.

"Oh, honey, I wish we could," Thorah half-whispered. Asêciwan and I exchanged a conspiratorial look. It was clear she had heard everything. I felt a rush of both embarrassment and pleasure at shutting her mom out of our unspoken understanding. It had always been that way with Asêciwan and me. She had grown in Thorah's body but the egg that made her came from mine. We were tied by blood and spirit and *iskwewak* fire.

"How are you doing on packing?" Thorah asked Asêciwan. "Can you give us two minutes and then I'll come check on your room?" Asêciwan inched down the hall in tiny backward steps, making it clear that she was resisting as much as possible while still following orders.

"Asêciwan, go!"

When her door clicked shut, Thorah said, "We're leaving tomorrow, with or without you."

"You're using her as a pawn." I said. "It's not fair. You heard her. She wants to stay too."

When Thorah stood up, her knees popped as if making a point. "I'm trying to save our lives."

I made my bed on the couch with a flannel sheet and my day clothes wadded into a ball. It was impossible to picture what it would mean to stay, to live alone, to abandon Asêciwan. We had already declared our departure to the authorities and surrendered the house for reclamation. Come tomorrow afternoon, the place would be scavenged for materials and stripped, with everything useful shipped to the New World. I lay awake, scrolling through pages of information about the underwater people on the New World, returning again and again to the phrases: *"Your circle is not round. All beings require more than one tide. Even desert animals live underwater."* That night I dreamed of drowning and woke gasping on the couch. I closed my eyes until sleep pulled me out like a tide, only to wake minutes later, parched and choking.

IT WAS STILL DARK when I checked through the items in my survival bag. I put coffee and eggs on as the first flash of sun cracked over the rooftops. A knock came from the front door. I used the doorsteel to open it, just wide enough for conversation. A round-bellied man stood with a crew of salvage workers.

"Morning. We got a lot to get to today, so we want to start outside early. That okay?" The salvage crews weren't supposed to arrive until the afternoon and I knew Thorah would be irritated that they were here. A friend told me that unscrupulous salvage unit bosses would pay city data workers for access to information on which houses were scheduled to be evacuated. The practice had led to crews poaching other crews' jobs. Bitter rivalries developed and there had been increasing reports of violence and salvage-gang murders. I nodded to the men that they could begin work, then closed the door.

Thorah didn't speak directly to me, but communicated through Asêciwan. The house shuddered and shook with the crew's activity outside. "Ask Mama if she has everything I told her to pack for the trip, or if I need to put some things in my bag," Thorah said.

Asêciwan looked questioningly at me. "Yes. No need to ask." I said. "I have everything from the list."

"Oh, good. I wasn't sure if Mama was still coming with us, so I had to ask."

"Yes. Of course I'm coming." I tried to level a look at Thorah but she was already out of the room.

Asêciwan spooned cereal into her mouth, keeping a wary eye on me.

THE STATION HAD THE YAWNING OPULENCE of its former days as a hub for trains of all kinds. For two hundred years, this spot connected the city to a network of rail arteries that cut every which way across the turtle's back, hauling lumber and produce, soldiers and grain, children and businessmen. Now that the trains had stopped and the station had been made over as one of two Canadian-controlled portals into the New World, the wide atrium was hushed.

On this day, the flow of people was orderly and calm. It was nothing like the hysteria of the first few weeks when the portal opened, where throngs pushed their way through the doors in an attempt to be the first to settle the New World. Journalists at the time had compared it, with enthusiasm, to a gold rush.

We arrived at the front of the line. A flashing red light indicated that we should approach the corner wicket. "Passports?" the woman asked. Thorah silently passed them under the glass barrier that separated the teller from us. "You didn't leave yourselves much time. Boarding begins in a few minutes."

"Kids. You know how it is," I ventured. Asêciwan raised an eyebrow.

The woman entered our names into her system. "Do you understand that once I check you in and confirm your passage as booked, you will not be allowed to rebook passage? This is a one-time one-way ticket."

"Yes, we understand." Immigration had taken this measure after too many people got cold feet and abandoned their seat in the portal's shuttle at the last moment. After the government lost hundreds of millions to half-full shuttles, they declared that each citizen would only be allowed one confirmed ticket.

"Please sign the declaration at the bottom of your receipt." The woman handed Thorah a sheet of instructions. "When you reach the New World, look for the family desk. It will be immediately to the right when you leave customs. It has a bright yellow awning marked with an arrivals sign."

The waiting area was a dingy grey box lined with linoleum tile. A single bench sat to one side as an afterthought. Signs on the walls asked that seats be given up for the elderly and disabled. Pregnant women were barred from entering the portal until their children were born. No one knew why. Looking around, I estimated that there were about four hundred of us waiting. Most stood with their regulation-sized bags, watching the wall-mounted screens deliver entertaining bits of information about the New World. *Did you know that residents of the New World experience a 40 percent reduction in asthma and respiratory illnesses, due to the improvement in air quality? Did you know that New Mount Everest is almost five hundred metres higher than Earth's Mount Everest?*

A voice came over the loudspeaker. "Good morning, passengers. We will now begin preboarding for those who require special assistance, including those with very young children. If you require assistance, please approach the shuttle gate."

"That's us." Thorah started moving to the front.

I looked down to take Asêciwan's hand, but she was gone. "Asêciwan?" I scanned the crowd of shuffling bodies for her purple T-shirt.

Thorah turned around and looked back for us. It took a moment for her to register Asêciwan's absence. "Where did she go?"

"I don't know."

The room was chaos. She could be anywhere. At one end of the room, opposite the portal gates, was a set of bathroom doors. "Stay here. I'll go look for her," I said, and pushed my way toward the bathrooms.

Inside, three teens huddled around a mirror, checking their looks. I crept low to get a look at the feet of the people in the stalls. They were all too big, and none had gold shoes. The voice on the loudspeaker came again. "We will now begin boarding for Elite class passengers only. General ticket holders are asked to stand behind the yellow line."

I dashed out of the bathroom and back into the crowd. The room was squeezed with tight-chested travellers pressing toward the gates. The shuttle itself was hidden by the long hallway that led beyond the gate. I shoved my way through the crush of bodies, ignoring the grunts and curses rising up around me.

Thorah was near the front, hands clenched around the handle of her suitcase. "Did you find her?"

I shook my head. "She's not here. I think she might have left the departures area."

Thorah gave a frantic glance at the line of people passing through the shuttle gates. "Shit."

"I'll check the main hall if you can talk to security."

Thorah grimaced, her eyes on the swarm of bodies moving through the doors.

"I ..." She pulled Asêciwan's passport out of the waist pouch that she always wore when travelling, and pressed it into my hand. "I'll save a place for us," she said.

"You're getting on?"

Thorah's eyes darted to the gate. "I don't want to go alone, but someone has to make sure they don't leave without you two."

"What if I can't get her in time?"

"You will."

She was lying. Every muscle in her body was clenched.

"Don't do this to us." I grabbed her sleeve and started pulling her away from the gates.

Thorah yanked herself sleeve away, recoiling as if she was being attacked by an animal. "I'll be here holding our spot. They won't leave. I'll make sure they don't." Her face was pinched. The tendons in her neck strained against her freckled skin as she clutched her bag to her chest.

"Thorah. They won't listen to you!"

She turned and let herself be swept toward the gate.

I moved against the tide of travellers, calling Asêciwan's name. I checked the bathroom two more times while the room emptied through the portal gates. With only minutes until the shuttle was scheduled to depart, I left the secure area, whirling into the station's expanse. In the lull between departures, the concourse was deserted, but for a tiny figure in purple waiting under the archway of the main doors.

I was out of breath when I reached her. Asêciwan looked up at me, her face giving up its stoicism with a little twitch beside her mouth. "What took you so long?" she asked.

"We have to go back. The shuttle is about to launch."

"No."

I glanced back to the station. "If we go to the desk, maybe we can get a message to Mommy that we might not make it."

She shook her head. Her steady brown eyes held mine, waiting for me to understand. I leaned in and listened to her with my body, willing her to say what I could not. Our breath rose and fell together like the drawing of tides. And then she blinked and turned away. The connection was cut.

Asêciwan took quick little steps down the carved granite stairway. She did not look back to see if I was behind her. I watched her go, thinking of Thorah strapped into her seat alone. A moment later, I let my feet carry me away from the station.

We walked to a platform that had been built as a viewing area for the shuttles to the New World. There was almost nothing to see when the shuttles left, but the few of us staying behind were still moved to gather. I held out my phone for Asêciwan to see the clock, and we counted down the seconds until takeoff. Her neck was taut and sweaty under my palm. At last, an old-time train whistle blew, and then a flash came from just behind the station. That was all. After a minute or two, the clusters of observers broke off and floated away.

"Can we go ask the lady if Mum really went through?" Asêciwan asked.

"Of course."

I TRIED TO APPEAR CASUAL when I asked the woman behind the glass whether or not Thorah had left on the shuttle.

"We only give that information out to family."

"She's my wife."

The woman squints at the screen, absentmindedly pushing her cuticles down with a fingernail. "Okay ... I can tell you that—yes, she did depart."

There was a bare flicker of pain around Asêciwan's eyes and then nothing. No tears. A wall.

I turned to Asêciwan. "She must have thought we were going to make it on the shuttle."

"No. She wanted to go," Asêciwan said. "She was afraid." I reached down for her hand, but Asêciwan was already striding purposefully toward the rectangle of light at the entrance of the station.

I had almost caught up to her when a voice behind me called, "Ma'am? Ma'am? You left your passports." I paused, then jogged back to the counter for the documents.

After the darkness of the station, the street was painfully bright. Heat ricocheted from the sun-blasted concrete. I put a hand up to shade my eyes, searching the empty roadway.

"Asêciwan?!" She was either gone or hiding. I tried to think where she would go. Her world, which once included the entire city and the faraway homes of our cousins, had been carved down to only a few short blocks. Now, there was only one place where she would run.

I retraced the steps we had taken earlier, feeling the soles of my shoes soften on the hot asphalt. The city was eerie without the everyday hum of people and traffic. The strange quiet seemed to amplify each small sound. The dry flap of a pigeon in a doorway, the clatter of an aluminum can rolling in a swirl of dust, a shout from somewhere up ahead.

"Asêciwan?!" I called again, but there was no answer. I reminded myself that it didn't mean anything. She knew enough to stay quiet and keep herself small in order to avoid danger. We both knew that as it got later in the day, there would be more people on the street, looking for who knows what.

Up ahead, a small group of men were peeking in the windows of cars in an abandoned lot. They had appeared as if summoned by my thoughts. I ducked into the alley and circled around, giving the men a wide berth. I had heard that there were roving gangs who scavenged anything of value to add to the stockpiles in their compounds. A pop of breaking glass and cheers echoed behind me. I walked faster. Private homes were still off-limits to the scavengers, but most commercial areas were a free-for-all. There had been rumours of women and children being stolen and sold, but it wasn't clear whether that was real or a story spread by the New World Government to try to encourage migration. Both seemed both likely, but in either case, it was always wise to avoid groups of men.

By the time I arrived home, an enormous metal container half-full of cracked gutters and scrap had been left squatting in front of the house. Without siding or windows, our home was no longer itself. It was diminished and strange, like a bird plucked of its feathers or a wolf without teeth. I found Asêciwan in the garden out back, hiding from the workers. They could be heard banging around inside, their laughter muffled as they yanked up floorboards and hammered the hinges from doors.

She crouched behind the Nanking cherry, pulling at the strangling vines that twisted into our yard from underneath the fence. I kneeled beside her and set to work tugging at the weeds. Her shoulders shook with tears. I put my hand between her shoulder blades as I had always done.

"Stop."

I pulled my hand back. Asêciwan yanked at a vine, pulling its ropy branching tendrils away from the fence, then following the length of it toward the house.

"We can't stay here, honey."

She spun around. "Why did you make me do that?" Her face was red, wet with sweat and tears.

"Do what?"

"You pretended you were gonna follow her. Even though you knew you couldn't."

"I was. I was going to follow her."

"No, you weren't! You left it to me! You made me choose so you didn't have to." She ripped at the vine, pulling up clods of dirt and orange calendula with it. "I hate you. I hate both of you." Asêciwan chucked the debris over the fence and curled up like a beetle, hugging her knees. A single sob broke free from her body before she could clamp down on it.

I stood there useless, feeling for the first time that she might not want me to comfort her. Knowing that I had hurt her in a way that could not be undone.

"Hey!"

I turned my head. The round-bellied man was standing at the back door, watching us. "You can't be out here anymore."

"It's our house. Back off." I spat.

He leaned against the doorjamb. "It's not. It's city property now. You'll have to find someplace else."

I rose to my feet and stalked toward him, claws out. His eyes flicked over me, assessing the potential for damage. "Get back in that house before I tear you a new one, mêwicisk!"

The man backed inside and slammed the door. "I'll give you one minute!" he called.

I crossed the grass to the back corner of the yard, where Asêciwan was curled up in the bare patch of dirt she had torn up. I reached down and held out my hand for her to take.

"Come. It's time to go."

Asêciwan slapped my hand away and stood up on her own. She brushed at the stains on her leggings, keeping her eyes fixed somewhere far beyond me.

The voices of the men rose up inside as they argued about what to do. Dark shadows crossed by the windows. They would be out here soon.

"Please, Asêciwan."

She squeezed her eyes shut and put her hands over her ears, as if by blocking out the world she could somehow make it different.

I heard the door click open behind me. Heavy feet dragged over the wooden boards of the porch. Asêciwan stayed rooted there, her face squeezed tight and quivering. There was a rustle of dry grass behind me. No more time. I lifted Asêciwan in my arms and swung around, rushing past the hard-eyed men. I squeezed through the narrow gap between our brick wall and that of our neighbours.

I burst out onto the sidewalk and sprinted down the street. Asêciwan was wailing now and pounding my back with her fists in a way that she hadn't done since she was four years old. Her heels flopped against my thighs. I ran down the middle of the heat-rippled pavement, not daring to look back until we were blocks away and Asêciwan had gone quiet and limp.

Parliament Street was dead, except for a corner store that had been open every day for twenty years straight. I set Asêciwan down stiffly on the pavement. She stood silently with her eyes down. I walked north, keeping an eye out for movement on the horizon. I could hear her trudging behind me. I stretched my arm for her to take my hand as we walked, but she left it to hang, an awkward invitation. After a few long moments, I let it drop.

We trekked silently through the hollowed-out city under the relentless midday sun. We were now without our luggage, without anything beyond each other. It occurred to me that in a year or two the streets would look completely different as plants and animals began to reclaim it. We were sleepwalking through a twilight time, after the unchecked human explosion, and before whatever came next. We zigzagged through the residential streets of Cabbagetown and up through Yorkville and the Annex, avoiding the ransacked storefronts of Bloor Street and those who scavenged there. Twice we encountered other wary stragglers. Each time, we kept to ourselves and they did the same. Throughout the long walk west, Asêciwan followed several paces behind. Her small whimpers and sniffles came like gusts of wind. I resisted the urge to hold her. It was odd that she hadn't asked where we were going—it had been more than a year since we ventured west of Spadina. I guessed she was too proud or too exhausted to care. She kept an even pace behind me, unwilling to either come closer or to be left alone.

Coming from the east, it was the flags that first rose up to announce that we had made it to High Park. Hot red and yellow Mohawk warrior flags flapped alongside rainbows and homemade banners with messages like THIS IS INDIAN LAND! AND UNITED NDN NATIONS! UNITED NDN SEXUALITIES! UNITED NDN GENDERS! Hundreds of them all flew high above a massive wall that surrounded a fortress of reclaimed materials. The wall itself was alive with flashing mirrors. Shards protruded like knives from the outside, making the barrier glitter in the afternoon sun. It was a thing of beauty and terror, designed so that anyone who tried to scale the wall sliced themselves open or drew the attention of the night watch with the sound of breaking glass. A hand-painted sign above the entrance announced our arrival at NAGWEYAAB ANISHINAABEK CAMP: RAINBOW PEOPLES' CAMP. A HOME FOR INDIGENOUS 2SLGBTTQI PEOPLE AND FAMILIES. I snuck a glance behind me. Asêciwan's face was inscrutable.

When we were within shouting distance, a small panel slid open and a voice called out:

"Aanii! Piish enjebayin?"

We stopped. They were Nish. I tried to remember something in anishinaabemowin, but my memory was suddenly gone.

There were whispers behind the fence, then a second voice tried, "Tansi! Awina kiya?"

The question filled me up. They spoke nehiyawewin. Our people were there and they wanted to know us. Asêciwan looked at me skeptically, then widened her eyes as if to say, *answer them, Mama!*

I knelt down beside Asêciwan and gathered her clenched fists between my palms. Her eyes flicked nervously toward the wall. I took a breath. "I'm sorry. I'm so sorry I didn't fight to keep us all here together."

Asêciwan's gaze snapped back to mine. At once, I could feel her listening. My words settled between us like a sheet. She clutched my hands harder.

"I miss her so much already," Asêciwan said.

I nodded, blinking. "Me too." She wrinkled her nose at me, showing me that she saw the tears building behind my eyes. Neither of us would allow ourselves to cry.

There was movement behind the wall. "Tansi! Awina kiya? Who are you?" The voice called out again. Asêciwan's eyes pleaded with me to respond. I kissed her on the forehead and pulled her close to me.

I directed my voice toward the faceless wall. "Em Callihoo nisihkason, egwa ..." I looked at Asêciwan.

She lifted her head, but stayed close to my chest, a layer of sweat between our bodies. "Asêciwan Callihoo nisihkason!" she called out. "Em Callihoo nikawi egwa Thorah Anderson nikawi. Amiskwaciy wâskahikan ochi niya. Tkaronto mêkwâc niwîkin." Asêciwan thrust out her chin proudly and glanced at me for approval. I nodded back, drunk on the sound of nehiyawewin on my daughter's tongue.

The person on the other side of the door was quiet. "Um, I'm still learning my language. What did you say? You're here with your mom?"

"She said her name is Asêciwan Callihoo. She said her mother is Em Callihoo and her other mother is Thorah Anderson. We're originally from Edmonton, but we live in Toronto. Pihtikwe ci?"

After a moment, a small door swung open. For the first time since that morning, Asêciwan and I walked side by side. Mother and daughter, two parallel planets.

AND THAT'S HOW THE ÂCIMOWIN, the story, was passed to me by my nôhkom. She lived back in the time before the reports came that life on the New World had fallen apart, before our protectors dismantled the portal so that it couldn't be engineered to bring the chaos from the New World back home to us. That was in a time before the plants and animals took back the city with their muscular roots and hungry young. It was before the High Law was signed by our matriarchs, shared responsibilities between the people and all our relations: the ones that walk on four legs, the ones that swim, the ones that soar in the air, the ones with leaves and branches, our grandfathers the mountains and our grandmothers the waters. Of course, the cycles of war and peace, love and heartbreak, hunger and feasting roll on, but with the understanding that we must always strive for balance. Above all, our circle must be round.

THE ARK
OF THE
TURTLE'S
BACK

JAYE SIMPSON

HAD BEEN STORING BIRCH SYRUP IN THE BASEMENT FOR SIX YEARS, mixing what little water there is with the syrup and trying to make it keep, when the International Water Ration Act of 2167 was made mandatory. Nishiime Dakib had gone off to the City around the same time I had come home from it. A fancy new private science sector had opened up and offered her a more than comfortable high-up position.

Dakib has been sending me hormones ever since one of the sweat-pourers said I was iwkekaazo, pretending to be a woman. The pills are expensive, and surgery is out of the question with the rationing upon us. We are getting even less water now, but we are used to it, our tap water having been unsafe to drink for nearly two hundred years.

The water in the plants is safe. I had been teaching folks in the community how to extract it safely and sustainably when the New Indian Agents set up camp wondering why we weren't dehydrated like the other Indians down south. I can't even remember how much blood was drawn from me, but they kept the questions coming and eventually left when we remained tight-lipped.

My house holds four of us: Axil, Giiweden, ashe, and me. Axil is a tall and lanky Michif man who shares a bed with me occasionally when my moon billows throughout my bones and causes a deep dry ache in my breasts and abdomen. I know it is wrong to lead him on like that; I just see no future raising children with him in this world. But an ache is still an ache. Together we collect syrup and keep the mining companies from taking Giiweden and ashe, the sometimes angsty young neechies in our home. The Moon settlement is always "recruiting" and, of course, the United InterCountry Senate is actively colonizing Mars after a successful terraform. I keep their hormone replacement therapy ongoing as the UICS has strict laws surrounding transgender individuals. Dakib always sends us six months of prescriptions every three months just in case the NIA come around.

DAKIB COMES HOME IN A TRANSPORT VAN when I am out among the Prairie Fire and ode'imin collecting the sweet and small hearts for preserves. She looks good, hair pressed and cheeks peach with powder. Manidoo, how I miss using blush, but how wasteful it is for me to crush these plants into dye to do so.

Dakib has this urgency, this drive, and begs us to pack up, telling us to gather only necessities and to leave the supplies and loved things behind. Dakib checks her phone constantly, breathes a sigh of relief when it took us only twenty minutes to gather our lives all up in two small suitcases, and groans when I bring my bundle, hand drum and all.

"*Nimisenh!* Sister! C'mon, we don't have time for this! The convoy is ready to leave and we're six hours to the City," she urges. I tut at her as I pull down the photo of Koko-Wahê from the wall to put in the bundle bag.

"Koko-Wahê didn't return home after five generations of displacement and kidnapping for you to rush us outta here," I snap at her.

"Koko-Wahê didn't run away from the Rez at the age of fourteen to go to the City to experiment with strangers and figure out their gender identity." Dakib waves her arms in a circle at my body, rushing me out the door. I let the words sting as Giiweden and ashe take their seats in the middle of the van, Axil getting in behind them looking concerned. The driver is youngish, from Six by the looks of it. He places a hand atop Dakib's shaking one as she slides into the front. I take a seat beside Axil. He slips his hand atop my lap and I let him kiss my shoulder.

"We meet up with the convoy at Auntie Leigh's, there's a team there for us. I can fill you in once there, but for now, please have faith in me, sister," Dakib states simply, forcing us into complacency, which by now we're used to out of fear of the NIA stealing bodies for their mining and "settlement" camps off planet. The truck rumbles, unaccustomed to the unpaved roads on the reservation. Giiweden grumbles about xyr graphic novel collection and being awake; xe is usually asleep during the day, especially in the heat of July. The van's air conditioning is on full blast and I can see Dakib still perspiring. Something else is up. Why go into the City? Metropolises weren't exactly the safest places for us as a very queer and very Indigenous family trying to hide from the NIA.

Auntie Leigh's convenience store is ahead of us, attached to the band office and the hall. I see similar looking vans idling with business-looking Indigenous folks standing nearby having what I can only describe as disconcerting looks on their faces. As our van pulls up, Dakib is already opening the door, shooting a warning glare at me, half asserting her dominance and half asking me to stay put. She should know better by now; Koko-Wahê did raise both of us.

I'm outside just behind her, grabbing her arm. "You tell me what's happening or I'll drop a damn house on you, so help me Manidoo," I hissed. She glares, an ocean swelling behind her brown eyes. She pulls her arm free and grabs me, pulling me away from both vans and other people.

"We're leaving, and soon. I'm gathering you all now so we can get it all done beforehand. The new settlements are ramping up, and I fear they'll take you no matter what now; Mars has a strong enough atmosphere with arable land. Who do you think is going to do that work?" At this point, tears are spilling from Dakib's eyes. "They already have the labour shuttles maxing out. The thing I've been working on is an exit strategy. We're getting off this damn planet before they take any more of us."

I clench my hands into fists, feel my nails dig crescents into my palms, hear a dull ringing in my ears. I sway like birch trees during a prairie black cloud storm. I try and ground myself, breathe in and out, on counts of four, until the ringing stops and my chest isn't heaving like angry earth sinking into the oceans. As my sight returns to me, I unfurl my hands and reach out to Axil, who looks quizzical. He gestures to Dakib and his shoulders rise in perfect synchronization with his sharp eyebrows. I shake my head, grunt a submission, and rest myself on his shoulder, this time letting my hand grip his and give two tight squeezes. He would make a good father if we had the chance to provide enough for a new generation. My reservations about him are clearly on my lack of ability to reproduce and the lack of opportunities to actually raise brown babies in a safer environment. Still, it's messed up, Axil always in the shadows of my love. He smells of seneca root and ode'imin juices atop his sweat. Giiweden is snoring now and ashe is falling into themself, which we have gotten used to.

Dakib slides into the van again, and this time, we peel out abruptly onto the road. The driver is quick and reflexive, his brow strong. I wonder if he is a lover of Dakib's. She always held several, but this one, thick braided and real ancestor-looking, may have made his way into her heart. Rare. I wonder if he is a Sixer or not. It would explain some of the tension between Dakib and him maybe even give insight into some of the very tangible sexual tension. Axil must notice my ponderings, as I am now seated upright and watching. *Nosy Auntie*, he would say, telling me to mind my own, stay out of their bingo hall.

Chhhhh, I'm nosy as all hell. "Dakib, who is this?"

She shifts uncomfortably, shoulders tensing. She, always uncomfortable with her older sister snooping into her life, looks out the window at the fading birch tree line transforming into prairie grasslands. I know I hit a nerve; she's holding her arm as if I injured her.

"Name's Archie. Kibby and I have been on this project since she was moved into the sector four years ago," he states. Dakib tenses at Archie saying *Kibby*; it sounds like a bedroom nickname. "Nice to finally meet you, Niichiiwad-*ikwe*," he finishes. The way he says *ikwe* gives away his Sixer heritage right away. They've been talking about me a lot by the sounds of it. He is trying too hard, awkwardly using *ikwe* to try and get me to like him. I already do. I wonder if he goes to sweats. Probably not. Not enough water left.

I WAKE, NOT REALIZING I HAD DOZED OFF, awkwardly smacking my head into Axil's. He grunts awake, lifting myself and him up. The van is parked. We're clearly underground. Dakib is typing rapidly on her cellphone while Archie is grunting into his. Giiweden and ashe are unsettled, and rightfully so. I clear my throat and Dakib turns in her seat to face me. "We'll be staying here for the next while. We have to run some tests, and honestly, stellar travel is a doozy."

I unbuckle, and my legs wobble as I climb out. Within minutes, we're unloaded and in an elevator going down. Dakib is shivering with what I can tell is excitement. I elbow her and grin. "Spill already, sis!"

"Okay, okay." She's grinning. "This facility is so large. I am so excited to finally show you around and share what I've been working on. We have a highly capable health team, and we can even get you into surgery by tomorrow, if that's something you still want? It's been a few years since you said so, but ..." She trails off.

Surgery. It's been seven years since I said that in a café back when I used to live in the City, and at least a year before I started harvesting water from the plant life back home. Surgery without enough clean water meant infection, failure, and even death. Surgery meant money, meant status, meant nobility, meant off-world. Surgery meant womb. The technology meant I could get pregnant, have beautiful brown babies form inside me. Tears well up. This time it's my turn for the ocean to breach behind my eyes. She grabs my arm. I must've been swaying, a habit I picked up after teenage trauma in the City. Giiweden looks at me, a deep yearning. I nod, seeing inipi fire and life in xyr eyes for the first time in a while.

"The both of you could be getting any surgery done tomorrow. We have a hydro-recycler and some pretty high-tech healing centres, and you'll be pretty well done healing before the Exodus!" Dakib is smiling, the elevator still descending. I face her, my eyes locking with hers. She straightens up because I have caught the word.

"Exodus?"

She begins to hold her arm and fidget nervously. Archie moves his weight from his left foot to his right.

"*Exodus*, as in numerous folks leaving *exodus*? How many?" I ask.

"Ni, a mass exodus. I can try to explain, but we have to go. The Senate is planning to swoop everyone up and force us into labour camps on the new settlements. They lied about trying to harvest the ice in comets and ice planets. They never had the infrastructure! Plus, the filtration needed would be beyond what is capable of the time. It will only be a matter of time before they come to take everyone capable from the Rez to work. The Moon's atmosphere is so successful that their oceans formed sooner than anticipated, and now they're filling the waters with formerly extinct species. But at what cost? Our brown bodies?

"The project we've been working on is based on a discovery from nearly one hundred and fifty years ago: a planet that can sustain life, a planet nearly four times the size of Earth, existing within a star's habitable zone! Over a hundred and thirty years ago, they sent terraformers and filtration systems to help prepare for our arrival, and it's ready now! Cities are already built to sustain us, animals and plant life already transplanted. There are buffalo, Ni! Buffalo!" Dakib is crying now with Archie's hand on her delicate shoulders. Axil is trembling, and ashe is clinging to Giiweden. Too good, this is too good to be true.

"Who did we colonize, Dakib. Who did we kill for this?"

A sob tears through her entire body, Archie embraces her, "No one, Ni! No one! There were no sentient life forms, a planet in its early stage of sustaining life, we just helped it along to get to a place where we can live!"

"Why are you sobbing." My questions are statements. A creeping ache blossoms in my chest.

"We don't have the supplies to take everyone, and—" She shudders as the elevator doors open to a concrete foyer illuminated in harsh fluorescents. We spill out.

Archie begins to speak, "We don't have the fuel for everyone. The size of the Arks makes the journey longer, and, well, we're using energy from Earth's kinetic core to fuel the trip. Upon takeoff, the core will cool almost entirely and cause significant damage to the planet. The magnetic field protecting Earth from solar winds and solar radiation will collapse and essentially turn Earth into the new Mars. The takeoff alone will cause enough damage that both the Moon and Mars settlements could be in trouble. The math can't confirm their safety, but at this point we need to leave. The amount of fuel needed to ensure the cryo-pods sustain between solar systems is large. This is all out of necessity."

"Necessity." I don't even realize I'm speaking. "Our people wouldn't leave her, and you know it. We would stay until her last breath and go with her. We are the caretakers, and if she dies, we die too."

I have squared up with Dakib now, like ancient earth upended by excavator maw. Face to face, I am an entire foot taller, and looking down, I see unfiltered rage looking back. Koko-Wahê's biggest flaw:

raising us both as stubborn rocks. But one of us is bound to break, very much like Earth after Dakib's "Exodus."

I AM THE ONE WHO BREAKS. For Giiweden and ashe, I break. For a chance at a future, a chance at tomorrow, a chance at children, I break.

It is in the recovery ward two weeks later in a bed beside Giiweden that I let myself collapse further. Sobs ripple through my shoulders like earthquakes, buckling Aki torn from her Nimama's breast, a dry wail billowing out of my throat like ribbon in prairie tornado. I am screaming, not from the procedure, but the sacrifice. I am trying to let go of Nimama Aki. I am trying to reconcile with this selfishness: letting Nimama die so I can carry children. Why, why fall into such old thoughts? Wasn't I happy without carrying child? Wasn't I content with my body? I had years ago come to terms with what I thought was loss. Shouldn't I be celebrating? This was what I always wanted, but at what cost?

Axil comes and goes, checks in on Giiweden often, leaves me to scream because he knows I will be done soon enough. ashe is worried, no matter how much Axil tells them, "Nimama-Ni is wailing, letting it all out, this is her Ceremony." Twice a day he brings me tea to soothe my bleeding throat. Dakib won't visit, my screaming clearly too much for her.

It is the third day when Giiweden starts crying beside me and whimpering, "Nimama, nimamaaaa, nimamaaaaaa." I stop and try to climb out of bed to reach xem, but my pain stops me. Still, one of mine is crying out for me. I continue to ignore the pain and stand. I crash to the floor and gasp, stomach tight. My hands claw at my abdomen. Xe is crying out for help as the sharp pains ricochet inside me, the ringing in my ears grows cacophonous, and my senses are ripped from me.

MY EYES ADJUST TO A BLUE LIGHT as I wipe the sleep from my eyes. I begin to sit up and I feel the familiar grip of Axil's hands on my arm and back. "Take it slow, zaagidiwin, slow." He guides me up. We are in a small medical room, the smell of metal and chemicals overwhelmingly present. I reach for my stomach, lift my medical gown and see fresh pink scarring down my hips, run my fingers down them, the nerves firing off with new sensation.

"ashe? Giiweden?" I cry out in confusion. My head is an actinoform cloud and I can feel my fingertips going numb. Axil is humming to me, reassuring me. I want to see Giiweden and ashe. I need to see them. I need to see Dakib too. As I stand up, Axil rushes to help me, pulling me up too fast. I sway like I used to in the City after a night out as the blood rushes through me. I laugh; standing feels very different now.

"There is something you should know, Ni," Axil says as I lean into him, let my hands brace his forearms, my hair in a messy braid between us.

"Hmm?"

"We had to take off a day after you fell in the ward. You were out for a week. We're on our way to the new planet." The room stops spinning. My heart stills as I search my spirit for Nokomis Moon. I lift my numb hands and place them on my chest, as if she were there. I sift through myself, coming to the realization that Nokomis Moon had long been hidden since her violent colonization a decade ago.

Axil guides me to a wheelchair. Although the newer technology in the earlier facility allowed for rapid healing, not practising the ability to walk has left me weary. He pushes us through the door, and I stop to feel the cool hum of the spaceship on my bare feet. The floor is a grated metal. I can feel us moving through space, braided delta rivers mixing with ocean brine, almost feeling like a freshly picked ode'imin tossed sneakily into hungry mouths. As we enter the corridor, I notice the simple rounded edges.

"How big is this?" I stammer.

"It's called an Ark. I think the Collective named it the Ark of the Turtle's Back. There are a hundred thousand pods and an atrium system that can sustain us all for twenty-five years if need be. The Ark is huge! There's a crew of five hundred or so, and we're in a fleet of five Arks." Axil fills me in, continuing to steer me toward some destination he seems to know. The corridors are surprisingly empty, the only sounds being an omnipresent hum and his footsteps.

We must've travelled for thirty minutes before we reach an elevator that whizzes us down (or at least what I think is down). He stops us as at a door marked C5-57 and places his thumb on a pad. The door hisses open to a small dwelling and four pods. Upon closer inspection, I notice each pod has a corresponding screen. I see our names, Nichiiwad Wahê, Axil Es, Giiweden Wahê-Es and ashe wahê-es. "Cryo," I stammer, placing my feeble left hand on my lower abdomen.

"This has really happened, hasn't it? We are actually gone? How far are we?" I move to stand with him, taking this opportunity to inhale his scent deeply. It isn't the same: our time in the City, and in the ship, has shifted him from raw seneca root and birch syrup to a faint scent of clean linens and his sweat. Still a comfort, for didn't he move from the City all those years ago to follow me back into the Wild? The Wild. I remember and ask, "What about Nimama Aki? Is there anything left?"

"Your sister and the team were correct. The liftoff of all the Arks at once caused the core to cool and lose a huge amount of kinetic energy. The Moon settlement is in a state of political chaos as their presidential parties were on Earth at the time. It may look like a complete overthrow since Mars has gone dark and they were the Military Stellar base. It was unfortunate, but the team said our survival was so important. The Moon is hanging on because of the gravitational pull, but they watched Earth's magnetic field shift and solar radiation destroy the surface. It's going to become another Mars and there aren't enough resources to seed the planet back."

I do not recognize myself. Being so far removed from the death of Nimama Aki, I feel like how I imagined Koko-Wahê when the police took her from our Big Koko all those years ago. I brace myself on Axil, grasping his thin shirt, and press into his chest. A cacophonous ache takes deep root in my breast and belly. He embraces me tightly.

I notice my bundle on a small shelf. I pull away from Axil, reaching for her. As I open the old brass clasp on the medium-sized briefcase, which is maybe a hundred years old, the faint smell of burnt sage and sweetgrass blooms. I pull my moon cycle medallion out and place it around my neck delicately. My and Dakib's kohkum once owned this, brought it with her to her first Ceremony in the Wilds. It has delicate blue beads and gorgeous detailed imagery of the Moon and her cycles. I lay a hand on the medallion and reach for the smoothed-out stone that I burn the medicine on. Axil's hand stops mine, and he looks at me and then at our living quarters.

"We should go to the Atrium. The air filters there can handle the smudging. Here, the sensors would probably flood us or something," he whispers into my ear. I pull a box of matches, the stone, a braid of sweetgrass, and bundle of white buffalo sage. The green shocks me back into the clinical and metallic world that encapsulates us. He leads me back to the wheelchair. Axil pushes me through the winding corridors and hallways. Eventually a door opens up into a large dome. Overwhelming at first, my eyes catch on the small garden thriving in a greenhouse in the centre. Axil moves us there. I see others, on different levels of the dome, moving around quickly, but return my attention to this smaller dome in the Atrium, the greenhouse.

Inside is a circle of aki and green. The green belongs to a birch, a red willow, and a cedar with grass and ferns collectively at their bases. Small rocks with moss and lichen are scattered in the greenhouse. I open up my bundle again and place some sage and sweetgrass in the stone and strike a black match alongside it. My hands are shaky when I lower the match into the bowl. The sage and sweetgrass are quick to light. I shake the match out and pull out a spotted owl wing fan from my bundle. I fan the small flames out and let the smoke tangle with the filtered air around me, curl around my hair, and seep into my skin. Axil inhales, presses his hands into my shoulders, and begins to pray. This is the closest I will be to the land that grew these medicines. The soil that birthed these medicines is gone, and there is nothing left but solar irradiated dust slowly freezing over.

I hear the door open behind us and Axil turns my wheelchair around. I face Dakib, Archie, Giiweden, and ashe. Giiweden is using a brace but walking toward me already. ashe is upon me, head in my lap, hugging me tight. I lay one hand on their head, let my fingers take root in their black curly hair. I reach for Giiweden and xe reaches for me. Axil guides xem to a nearby chair and we fall into each other. Dakib and Archie watch, and I look up. She smiles weakly. I give her a once-over, note her new uniform: a black one piece with a utility belt. She looks good, especially since Archie is in an identical outfit.

The smudge lingers. ashe and Giiweden let their limbs flow through it, bringing the smoke into them. Dakib and Archie sneak closer and closer, until I gesture to them. Archie sighs with relief and, surprisingly, Dakib undoes her bun and falls into the Ceremony quickly. She moves the lingering smoke into her and turns around for me to brush her back and fan her off. This is growth, for someone who ran from inipis and pipe ceremonies. She is allowing me to practise, and with her. Giiweden starts humming a Nokomis song, and ashe keeps beat with their hand on my lap. Axil nods to growing drumbeat. This sliver of Ceremony feels so natural, our songs so close, our medicine swirling around us. I do not want this to end, but Dakib steps back and returns her hair to a tight bun. We look like opposites, me still in a pale blue medical gown and my hair in a messy braid down the left side of my neck.

"All of the others are in their cryo-pods, where they will sleep for the next fifty years." Dakib breaks the silence of the Ceremony, bringing us back into reality, a giant spaceship hurtling through the ether of space and time. "You and Giiweden will need to stay awake for three months for healing. We will be awake for the duration, the crew and the health team. But after you and Giiweden are cleared, it's into the cryo-pods for all of us." She finishes and turns around quickly, exiting with Archie following.

"She's still a robot, eh?" ashe says, breaking the silence left by Dakib's cold exit. I let out a laugh that grows quickly. ashe looks up at me, smiling. Axil chuckles and Giiweden giggles, all of us breaking into laughter and trembles, our bodies moving with our collective music.

THE DOCTOR TYPES SOME THINGS into the glass screen before her and smiles. "Healing is complete. The cryosleep will freeze everything for now, so you will be okay. Dakib has approved you and your family's preparation for travel. We will do an immediate check-in once we enter the orbit of the new planet. It's been an absolute pleasure, Nichiiwad. I have already cleared Giiweden. We will be placing you under in twenty minutes. I will see you in just under fifty years." She watches me as I stand up and begin to walk out. I am greeted by Axil, his smile foolish and sly. We embrace with our foreheads touching.

"I want twins, Axil. I want babies on babies. I want brown babies. I want fat brown babies. I want them to speak the languages. I want them to know our songs. I want them to have everything Koko-Wahê tried to give me and Dakib. I want everything for them that we couldn't have. I want this, with you. I can't have this without you. I have been so awful, so awful and so cruel. You have always been there, even as I've been so distant to you."

He nods, grins, and pulls me along the hallway and pauses just before entering our quarters. I want this to last forever: us, entangled, holding tightly onto everything we have loved before we entered the void. He stops and reminds me that we should be changing into long-term pajamas for sleep. ashe and Giiweden are already inside with an attendant who will check vitals and place us into our pods. The bedding in the pods is cool and soft, like fancy memory foam mattresses, but made from a gel-like substance. As the attendant begins to close my pod, I raise my hand, stopping her. A small silver curl escapes her bun as she is jolted to a stop.

I ask, "How do we build a relationship with this new planet?"

She laughs. "I would assume like all consensual relationships: we ask them out."

I smile, nodding as she closes the pod. I whisper a prayer and look over at Axil, ashe, and Giiweden, all of whom are already asleep.

"Tomorrow will be kinder," I whisper as I am swept into the rushing river of my dreams.

HOW TO SURVIVE THE APOCALYPSE FOR NATIVE GIRLS

KAI MINOSH PYLE

1. I'm writing this down so I don't forget. I want to be one of those seventy-year-old women with their photo albums and old diaries, the ones who can recite stories from when they were children or from even further back. Migizi used to say things like "we are future ancestors" all the time.

I think about that a lot.

2. I started thinking about this the other day and it occurred to me that maybe what we need is an instruction book. *How to Survive the Apocalypse for Native Girls*. Or maybe, *An Indigenous Futurist's Guide to Life*. The first one was my idea, because that's what I am, a Native girl surviving the apocalypse (that's what Migizi liked to call it). But then my kookum told me about this old movement from when she was my age. She said that a long time ago, Black people invented something called Afrofuturism. The Afrofuturists imagined the future, but not just any future. They imagined ways that they could get free, ways they could hold their ancestors and descendants in the same hands. And my kookum said that other Indigenous people thought this was a beautiful thing, so they began calling their imaginings Indigenous futurisms.

My kookum said that sometimes there were border wars. Sometimes, the border wars were literal. I know this because my girlfriend Shanay is Black and Anishinaabe and the Nation didn't want to let her grandma in when she was little, because she didn't have papers. Apparently papers used to be very important.. Migizi, who always knew about history things even though they weren't even old, said now we have Kinship instead, but I don't think Migizi always liked Kinship either because sometimes they would argue with council members about it. My kookum won't tell me but I'm pretty sure that's why Migizi had to leave. Because they argued too much.

3. Here is my first instruction: when the apocalypse happens, make sure you bring your kookum. Mine is named Alicia. She doesn't have an Anishinaabe name, because when she was born they were only starting to get them back. You're going to want your kookum when the apocalypse happens because kookums know everything. Mooshums do too but they can get bossy and think they're right all the time, like the council does. Kookums secretly *know* that they're right all the time, but they also know that different teachings are correct.

Oh—maybe I should make that another instruction. That one is important.

3.5. Different teachings are correct. My kookum says she learned this from an old lady she knew as a kid, a woman from Nigigoonsiminikaaning who taught her the language and also how to set snares, which is really useful after the apocalypse. My kookum named me in her honour, Nigig, after the community she came from. The woman from Nigigoonsiminikaaning told my kookum (and lots of other people) that everyone is taught in a different way. You can't say that one teaching is the only correct one, because then you would be putting down someone else's teaching.

I think this is a good instruction, but sometimes I wonder about it. Migizi told me that a long time ago, around the same time when Indigenous futurism was invented, there were the Skirt Wars. They weren't actual wars, unlike the border wars, but people argued a lot then, about whether Native girls have to wear skirts to ceremony, and how 2spirit people should act during ceremony. Migizi always looked really upset by the Skirt Wars stories, and I don't blame them. They're 2spirit, too, even though I am ekwewaadizid and they are eniniiwaa-dizid. I wonder if anyone ever told Migizi that they had to wear a skirt to ceremony.

4. Maybe I should start off with what I know. If someone (such as a Native girl living after the apocalypse) finds this, how can I guarantee they know about what happened? Will they know about the border wars and the hungry years? Will they know about Kinship and about the council?

I just realized, they won't know who Migizi was. Oh.

5. I've decided that everything is too much. Also, I'm not sure that I know everything. So I will ask my kookum later. But I can tell you (the future Native girl reading this) about me. I was born to the Crane Clan during the Bakadeng, what people who speak English call the hungry years. I was born near the end of the Bakadeng, which started when my parents were young adults after the other kind of borders collapsed, the one they used to call the Medicine Line. As a kid I used to look at the old papers, all of them written in English, that my family had to carry around when they crossed those borders. It was my way of remembering my parents, who died when I was only a baby. Now I travel around Anishinaabewaki with my kookum, with no papers needed at all. I'm sixteen years old and when I grow up I'm going to be a storyteller like Migizi.

Migizi. That's the name of my best friend. Migizi was born before me by many years, but we've been friends as long as I can remember. When I was little Migizi used to tell me stories about 2spirit people from a long time ago. I used to think they knew every Anishinaabe 2spirit who ever lived.

Migizi was the one who helped me realize that 2spirit is a thing I could be. That I could be a Native girl—that I could even be a Native girl who loves other girls! What a wonderful discovery.

Not everyone liked Migizi as much as I did. They were the one who gave me this book, though, so I feel like I should explain about them. When Migizi got their new name, the elders decided to name them after Eagle. I don't know why they did that, but it always reminds me of this story about Eagle. You know, the one where Eagle flies around the earth every day to make sure there is at least one person putting down tobacco and being a good person? See, Migizi has this thing about them. They are trying so hard to always be a good person that it makes everyone around them want to be a better person too.

6. Here's an instruction: Love is good. Today I saw Shanay again for the first time in a few months. My kookum and I travel around so she can do ceremony for people, and also because she's the gossip of Anishinaabewaki and has to know everything about everyone so they can ask her what's going on far away in Baawitigong or Onigamiinsing or Obishikokaang. Shanay just lives in Miskoziibiing all the time because she's studying with her grandma to become a doctor. Shanay's grandma is one of the best doctors, because she was trained both Anishinaabe-way and in one of the old universities before the borders broke down. She likes to joke that it's a good thing the apocalypse happened, because that way she didn't have to pay off her student loans, which were apparently a thing that, like money, used to be a big problem for people.

So I saw Shanay and I was reminded about Love. Love is part of Kinship laws—it is the Kinship laws. Of course in reality Kinship is just as much about hating each other and messing each other up as it is about loving each other, but without Love there wouldn't be any Kinship at all.

When I saw Shanay today, she said, "Wow, Nigig, I almost forgot how gorgeous you are." I blushed a lot, could feel the warmth in my face. Then she pulled me into her arms and kissed my nose and my cheeks and finally my mouth and I melted.

That's Love.

7. I met Shanay at the 2spirit youth potluck in Miskoziibiing that Migizi took me to a while after we had the feast announcing I was a girl. She sat down in the chair next to me and gave me a little smile, and we introduced ourselves to each other.

"I'm from here originally, but my kookum and I were living in Onigamiinsing last year," I told her. Then I corrected myself. "Well, Baawitigong a little bit too. Oh, and before that, Nogojiwanong."

"Wow, you've been all over!" Shanay smiled ruefully and sighed. "I've lived here my whole life. My grandma's dad was from the south, outside Anishinaabewaki, and I've always wanted to learn about other places, but the truth is I get nervous even when I go too far outside Miskoziibiing for fasting."

"Aww, well, that's because you're fasting, you're all alone in the woods!" I reached out a hand and touched her shoulder. She blinked for a second, her face a little flushed, and I quickly pulled away, not sure what had gotten into me. I coughed, and continued, "Travelling can be lonely too. But when you're doing it with someone you love ... that's when it's the best."

As she opened her mouth to reply, Shanay was drowned out by the sound of Migizi on the hand drum. Around us everyone was circling up for a round dance. I stood up, and made an awkward gesture at the crowd. "You wanna ...?"

For a terrifying second I thought she might say no. But then Shanay got up and, as she headed toward the circle, she turned just enough to grab my hand and tug me along with her.

We danced every song that night, and my hand never left hers, the warmth spreading from the place where we touched throughout my whole body. We've been inseparable ever since.

8. Shanay and I talked for a long time after I got back to Miskoziibiing. I told her about this book that I'm writing and she had some suggestions, so here are her ideas.

SHANAY'S SUGGESTION #1: "Everyone has ancestors, but not everyone knows theirs." This is very wise, I think. I know most of my ancestors going way back because of the old papers from the Nation and from the government that existed before the Nation, but because of the border wars, some people don't have those records, like Shanay. And some people, like Migizi, don't have kookums to tell them the stories.

SHANAY'S SUGGESTION #2: She thinks I should talk more about Kinship. Shanay is a little bitter about Kinship, like Migizi, except she has even more reason to be bitter since her grandma was originally rejected from the Nation. See, when the borders broke, people decided that Kinship should be our main law instead. Except the problem was that Kinship means different things to different people. And sometimes people who should see each other as kin, inawemaagan, reject each other. That's what happened to Shanay's grandma, until one of the clan leaders adopted her.

SHANAY'S SUGGESTION **#3**: "You talk a lot about Migizi." That's what she said. I think she means I talk too much about Migizi. When she said this to me, I felt my face harden. It was the opposite of melting.

"What is wrong with talking about Migizi?" I asked her. She made an expression that was sad and disappointed and fond at the same time.

"Nigig," she told me. "You have to move on. Talking about Migizi all the time isn't going to bring them back."

"Migizi isn't dead," I said to her. Her face became pinched like she had bitten a lemon (a fruit I tasted once recently which is very tart). Then she rubbed her eyes very hard and when she looked up again I could see that there were some tears there. Migizi was my best friend but I forget sometimes that other people loved them too.

Shanay took my hand in her hand and squeezed. "Nigig," she said again. "You have to learn to live with what is here *now*. You have to just *be*."

9. Sometimes Love is not so good. When that happens Kinship can sometimes help, and sometimes it can hurt. That is what happened to Migizi.

I still don't know when Migizi was born, but I know they came of age around the time I was born, during the Bakadeng. We call that time the hungry years not just because people often went without enough food, but also because there was often another kind of hunger. The kind of hunger that causes people to do terrible things: wiindigo hunger.

Here is a teaching about wiindigoog for you: Wiindigoog are more than just cannibals. They are possessed by a hunger that only increases every time they try to fill it. That hunger can be for anything—food, drugs, sex, love, but most of all, power. Migizi's parents were the kind of people who were infected by the wiindigo spirit of the Bakadeng. Migizi never talked about it, not even with me, but they had scars on their hands and arms like burn marks. They wore long sleeves to cover them most days, but they stood out if you noticed them, still faintly redder than the brown of Migizi's skin.

Once, when I first met Migizi, I asked them where they grew up. Migizi's eyes went a little blurry, like they were looking far into the distance. Their breath turned shallow and their whole body tensed. They reminded me of how deer react when they spot you in the woods with a gun. I stood still, as though my own sudden moves might scare Migizi just like one of those deer.

"A place that doesn't exist anymore," Migizi said finally, their breath starting to deepen again.

"Where did it go?" I asked. I was just a kid and didn't know how to read the words in Migizi's face.

For a long moment I didn't think Migizi was going to answer me. They were still staring ahead, not looking at me, their lips held tightly shut. But then they said, very quietly, "It was consumed by wiindigoog." And they refused to say anything else.

It wasn't until I began to realize that I was not the boy everyone thought I was that Migizi told me more. When I told them I was going to talk to my kookum to see if we could have a feast for me being a girl, Migizi's jaw became tense and they were silent for a minute.

"Nigig," they said to me, "I'm going to tell you something, and I don't want to scare you. But it's something you should know about."

Which made me scared just on principle. But then Migizi told me. They told me about how they had asked their parents, as a young teenager, if they could cut their hair and ask an elder for a new name, one that didn't end in kwe. They told me about how their mother had cried and their father had screamed, how they had left in the dead of night. They told me how the people they had grown up with, their close and extended kin, had one by one shut their doors in Migizi's face, even though it was winter in Anishinaabewaki.

"I survived that night," Migizi said slowly. "I went west to Miskoziibiing, found another 2spirit who showed me safe places to sleep."

"Why are you telling me this?" I whispered.

Migizi reached out suddenly, wrapped an arm around me, and smooshed me against their shoulder. "I just want you to know, Nigig. I want you to know that for some people, inawemaagan doesn't include people like me and you."

I didn't want to understand then. "But the Kinship laws—"

I could feel Migizi shake their head. "Kinship is a two-sided coin, Nigig. You always gotta ask yourself, who is being excluded here?"

10. Instruction inspired by today: Watch those in power carefully. That is what my kookum always tells me when she makes me attend council even though I'm not old enough to participate yet. I've been going since I was little. That's where I first saw Migizi, actually. They were arguing with the council, of course, even back then when they were just my age.

Today Shanay, her grandma, my kookum, and I all went to the western door council meeting. It was my first time at council without Migizi, and I tried not to think about that too hard. Shanay's grandma gave a report on the situation in the Miskoziibiing hospital, and a lot of people frowned while listening. Shanay's hand gripped mine tightly the entire time. I didn't miss the looks a few people gave Shanay and her grandma when they walked in. A little tension in the room flowed out when Shanay's grandma started talking—she is one of the few people of my kookum's generation who grew up speaking Anishinaabemowin, and her accent is flawless. Still, my other hand, the one not holding Shanay's, curled around the edge of my seat until my knuckles started to hurt. The news about the hospital wasn't so good.

One of the council members, a woman from Eagle Clan, stood up after Shanay's grandma. Her voice filled the room even without shouting.

"Perhaps supplies wouldn't be so low," she said, looking straight at Shanay's grandmother, "if you weren't treating every single stranger who comes to your door."

There were quiet gasps, but just as many people seemed to be nodding. The word she used for stranger was meyaagizid—someone who was not kin.

Shanay's grandma looked right back at her and said in her forever-steady voice, "Since it was established, the Miskoziibiing hospital has *always* made it our policy to treat *all* who need our services. Whether they are inawemaagan or meyaagizid."

The Eagle Clan woman's face was stormy. "Policy it may be." Her tone was slow, deliberate, and a little vicious. "But all must still abide by the laws of Kinship within Anishinaabewaki."

"Kinship does not exclude kindness toward strangers," my kookum said loudly, standing up next to Shanay's grandma. The Eagle Clan woman's frown deepened. I think she realized she was facing two respected women who were her elders, and that the very Kinship laws she was arguing for insisted she defer to them. She sat down hard and began whispering furiously to the council members next to her.

My kookum leaned over then and said very low in my ear the instruction that I just shared: Watch those in power carefully. That's why I wrote this down. And my kookum was right, because writing it down made me remember that Migizi was from Eagle Clan, and the woman who argued with Shanay's grandma was the one in charge of their fate.

11. Sometimes, when it's the apocalypse, you have to just do things for yourself.

My kookum won't tell me about what happened to Migizi. When I ask, she gets a very pained expression on her face, and refuses to speak about it. But once I saw the Eagle Clan woman and the way she talked to my kookum and Shanay's grandma, I knew what I had to do.

After the council meeting was over, I told Shanay and my kookum that I was going to the bathroom. I followed the Eagle Clan woman out of the council chamber and into a back hallway. I guess I wasn't great at being sneaky, because as soon as I shut the door (as quietly as I possibly could) she turned around and put her hands on her hips. "Well?"

My tongue felt thick and knotted. She took this as a sign to start talking. "You want to give me a lecture too, like those relatives of yours?" she snorted, and anger started to get hot inside me at her condescending tone. My fingers pressed into my palms, and I could feel my nails leaving little marks in my flesh. "Please. I have better things to do than listen to a child's righteousness." And she started to turn away.

"Wait," I finally said. "*Wait*." She kept walking. "I just want to know what happened to Migizi!"

The Eagle Clan woman stopped dead. She turned back around to face me slowly. Then she walked right up to me, and bent down until face was inches from mine. "What did you say?"

I swallowed the dryness in my throat. "Migizi. My friend. I want to know what happened to them."

There was a funny glint to her eyes as she studied my face. "That's right, they did have a little pet, didn't they?" She smiled, sweet and slimy. "Migizi is gone, child."

"You can't exile someone just because you don't like them," I said hotly. "Kinship—"

"Kinship is exactly the reason why that freak had to be gotten rid of," she spat. "Do you even know what they did?" I blinked and the woman's eerie smile came back. "You don't, do you? Ah, Migizi, Migizi. They were always trying to pick a fight over the Kinship laws. I wondered for a long time why they were so hostile about that—but then when you've murdered your entire family, I guess your only hope is to overthrow the norms of Kinship."

I stood there, slack-jawed. "What?"

The Eagle Clan woman pulled back from me a bit, looking ever more satisfied. "You heard me. Migizi slaughtered their own inawe-maaganag. Set their own house on fire, left the entire village to burn. And ran like a coward."

There was nothing I wanted in that moment more than to get as far away from the Eagle Clan woman as I could and never see her again. But my entire body had become too heavy to move. "You're lying!"

"Look, I'm sorry." She shook her head. "That grandmother of yours should never have let them come near you. But I promise you, Migizi is gone by now."

In Anishinaabemowin, the word maajaa can mean two things. Usually, it means someone has left, gone somewhere else. But other times, it means—

"They're dead, child. No one survives long outside the protective network of the Nation." She grimaced. "Why do you think so many meyaagizijig want to come here, anyway?"

I was shaking all over by then. My mouth wouldn't work properly. After a minute of waiting, the Eagle Clan woman shook her head again, muttered to herself, and walked away. I watched her go all the way down the hallway before I felt like I could move again.

12. I always knew terrible things had happened during the Bakadeng, and before, during the border wars, and even before that, when powerful states ruled the world. My kookum sometimes would go fuzzy when she talked about it, would get tears in her eyes or shaky hands. Especially when I was little, these moods scared me, and I would try to comfort her with rabbit stew or a funny story. It was only as I got older that I realized that there is only so much you can do to help.

Shanay had whispered to me once that when she grew up, she wanted to specialize in medicine for people whose minds and hearts were in pain, like my kookum and Migizi. Maybe someday she will invent just the right combination of food and laughter to cure sadness.

"Hey," Shanay said when I told her what the Eagle Clan woman had said. "You don't know what happened. We don't know the full story. You remember Migizi's scars. Someone did that to them."

I froze, remembering how much of Migizi's skin was covered by those burns, and Shanay grabbed my hand.

"Nigig, when I go with my grandma to give people medicine, sometimes they are hurt really bad. And sometimes ..." She had a peculiar tender look on her face. "Scars aren't the only marks that violence leaves behind."

"Why wouldn't they *tell* us, then?" My voice broke as I half-shouted the words. Shanay pulled me into her arms and I curled into her, tucked my head against her neck, and tried to breathe.

"Maybe," she murmured against my hair, "Migizi was just trying to protect us."

When I was holding Shanay like that, I didn't say anything else. But I'm writing the truth down here. And the truth is, when you're a Native girl living in the apocalypse, there's only so much anyone can protect you from.

13. I'm crying as I write this. I don't know what to do. I don't have any words of wisdom for you, future Native girl surviving the apocalypse. What is there to say when you're going to lose yet another person who you love most in the world?

Back up. Deep breath.

Early this morning, Shanay came to me in tears, panicking. Her grandma came in close behind her, looking for my kookum. As they talked, Shanay told me what had happened.

The council said Shanay's grandma broke the laws of Kinship in her work at the hospital. They say she prioritized meyaagizijig over our inawemaaganag. They said her Kinship ties were always suspect, since her father was not Anishinaabe. They said she and her descendants had forty-eight hours to leave Anishinaabewaki. Forever.

"It's not fair," Shanay sobbed against my shoulder.

"Shh," I whispered, stroking her hair lightly. Behind us I heard my kookum's voice raise as she cursed out the council members one by one. "We'll figure this out," I said. I was buzzing, ready to take on the council myself. "You're not leaving. I promise."

I said those things and I meant them, but I don't know how I can possibly make them true.

14. *Dear Nigig,*

When you find this, I hope you are not too angry with me. We've known each other for so long, and there's so much I still haven't told you. Not because of you, see, but because I'm still scared. Scared that the wiindigoog have followed me even here.

I wish I could tell you that what they will say about me isn't true. It is. But it's not the whole story. What does it mean to break Kinship with someone who has never regarded you as their kin? I know you and Shanay have seen the burns on my skin (you're not as subtle as you think, my friend). The people who did that to me should have claimed me, should have treated me with love.

The night I left they tried to burn me. They were laughing, telling me if I wanted to be a faggot so bad I should burn like one. Nigig, I was so scared. I fought them and I ran and I didn't look back to see what happened. I didn't want it to happen like that, but I'm not sorry I got away. Maybe that makes me the monster they think I am. I don't know anymore.

They will try to tell you that they exiled me, that there is no way to survive outside the Nation. Don't believe them, Nigig. Don't believe that the "strangers" who make their way into our lands are without their own ways to survive.

You've always been so strong, Nigig. Trust yourself. Hold the ones you love close. I know you'll find your own way.

53.713287, -114.393061

15. I guess I lied that day when I promised Shanay she wouldn't leave. But I didn't know what I know now. There's more to the world than what I've seen.

Migizi is out there somewhere. My kookum says she knows how to read the numbers they left me. I'm going to find them, and Shanay is coming with me. We're stuck together, her and me. I'm not losing her, not ever.

I told her that this morning as we packed our bags, and her eyes closed but no tears fell.

When it came time to leave, the four of us—Shanay, her grandma, my kookum, and me—gathered together in the kitchen. My kookum looked at me for a long time.

"I'll see you again," she said at last, not even a waver in her voice. When I started to protest, she held up a hand. "Someone needs to stay here to fight the council. To find a new way to hold our people together."

My body was heavy and I felt more tired than I had ever been in my entire life. I thought about every time my kookum had made me lead her through the trails of Anishinaabewaki, the ways she had showed me how to check the trees and stars to find my way. I thought, too, about the ceremonies she taught me and the ways to talk to people in new places, how to make meyaagizijig into inawemaaganag. I didn't know what world Migizi was living in now, the world outside Anishinaabewaki, but as I saw the steadiness in my kookum's gaze, I felt like maybe I was ready for this.

There was no way to say all that, so I just nodded instead. She reached for me and tugged me close. I heard Shanay sniffle and her grandma murmur her reassurance.

"Giga-waabamin miinawaa," I said, repeating my kookum's goodbye back to her. "I mean it."

She smiled at me. "I know, my little Nigig. Bring back some good stories for me."

16. So here we are, at the edge of Anishinaabewaki. Right where you come in.

I knew what I had to do the minute I saw you there in the crowd of people protesting the council. I could hear your voice through the singing and slogans. And then you looked at me, and you smiled a little and gave me that nod that says, "I see you."

Maybe this, too, is Kinship.

So I'm passing this on to you. If I know my kookum, there will be a lot of changes happening in the Nation soon. And you might need the help of an instruction guide for a 2spirit girl living in the apocalypse.

I don't know if or when I will come home. Or if home will even mean the same thing to me once I've left. But I hope that you'll read what I've written here and remember the stories of the people that I love. Shanay, my kookum, Migizi. And when you've read it all, you can add stories of your own.

I don't know your name. I don't know who your kin are. But I know you're worth it, niijiikwe. And I know now that the only way to survive the apocalypse is to make your own world.

So let's get started.

ANDWÀNIKÀDJIGAN

GABRIEL CASTILLOUX
CALDERON

THE ELDERS HAD TOLD HER STORIES ABOUT THE WORLD THAT WAS. Stories about a mother who was earth. Stories about how the ones in power killed her. Others said the stories were lies. The world was always grey and concrete, steel and sorrow. They were born into it, so were their children. The only reason elders told stories was in order for the memory markings to appear. No one in the village knew why. However, when someone shared a story and you truly listened, listened with all your heart, by the end, strange red markings would appear on your skin, like tiny scratches that fell into a pattern no one could discern. When you touched one, words would appear in your head, and you would repeat the story back, verbatim, as if you were the one who shared it in the first place.

No one knew why only the people in the village had the markings, or where they came from, or what they were for—but the people in power did. Therefore, one day, on the most special day, the day when the young ones go through their adulthood ritual and hear the creation story to receive their first markings, the ones in power attacked. They left no one alive.

Or so they believed.

A′TUGWEWINU AWOKE STARTLED; her breath coming in short gasps and sweat beading her brow. She quietly got up from her pallet on the floor so as not to disturb the bed's other resident. A'tugwewinu sat in the adjacent room, on the edge of the wall, where there was a hole in it big enough to fit her comfortably. The air was stiff and hot. No wind from the open wall to soothe her blistering skin. The sky was an orange glow with a dull light emanating from the centre. The sky was always orange. Sometimes the dull light would be brighter, other times gone completely. Regardless, it was always hard to see. She looked down at her arm, skin bronzed and grimy, and softly rubbed the markings there. They were fresh from a merchant telling her about a story his grandfather had passed to him.

Gently she felt fingers touch her nape and Bèl's gentle voice murmured in her ear. "When did those marks happen?"

"This morning."

Bèl's strong hands moved her body around to face their owner. A'tugwewinu looked into warm, immeasurably deep eyes like onyx and smooth, dark lips shaped into a quiet smile.

"Do you want to hear the story?" A'tugwewinu asked.

A nod. Bèl's hand grasped hers, graceful fingers callused from fighting that tugged her away from the harsh sky and the arid air, back to the protection of their little pallet nest.

"Your turn," A'tugwewinu whispered, holding her arm out.

Bèl looked at her solemnly before turning their gaze to the fresh markings with true intent. Those scarred fingers gently pressed on them, putting into the touch the need to listen and learn. The markings triggered, sending a cold snap into A'tugwewinu's head. Everything was silent, until suddenly, word after word barraged her senses. She took a deep breath and opened her mouth.

"It was a bright cold day in April, and the clocks were striking thirteen."

SHE SAT UNDER *the metal overhang near the outskirts of the village. It was her little place, only those closest to her knew it. She fiddled with the hem of her ribbon shirt. The frayed edges wrecked wonders to the nerve endings under her fingernails. Footsteps approached as A'tugwewinu looked up and saw her mother come closer.*

"Hey," she said as her mother sat next to her.

"Hey," her mother replied.

They both sat silently for a bit, staring out into the brown and dappled grey hills around them.

"The boys made fun of Kokomis' shirt. They said I'm a girl and girls shouldn't wear men's clothes. They said I'm wrong."

Her mother crooned. She gently grasped her face. "When you were born, your Kokomis held you in his arms and he looked at me with tears running down his face because he had been waiting his whole life for another îhkwewak like him, and there you were, I gave birth to you, and I was never more grateful for anything else in my life. You are a gift, Winu. And people are often jealous of gifts that are not for them."

A'tugwewinu tossed her arms around her mother and held her tightly. For a moment, it was serene. Then her mother began muttering in a strange language, something she did when visions would consume her. A'tugwewinu withdrew her embrace and looked into the white pupilless eyes of her mother, her mouth moving constantly, strange sounds and gurgles spewing forth. Suddenly, her mother's hand shot out and grasped her arm, in her mind she was assaulted with images, fire, the faces of people she knew screaming in agony, moving metal machines with weapons that killed thousands. "Run," her mother demanded. "Run, toward the east, as fast as you can. Hide when you hear anything. Run!" With her final decree, she released her death grip on her child.

A'tugwewinu gasped as the images stopped. She looked at her mother whose pearl pupilless eyes had returned to a beautiful roasted brown. Tears fell down her face. Her mother nodded at her once. With her final salute, A'tugwewinu turned and ran.

It wasn't until a few hours later that she saw the fire rise to the sky with billowing clouds of ash and heat where her village once stood. The roar of hundreds of villagers' spirits rose from the earth. She loosened her cries of anguish for all that she loved was gone.

AFTER THE STORY WAS COMPLETE, both lovers fell back into peaceful sleep. In retrospect, the morning could have been serene. It could have been a tender, warm awakening, filled with lengthy kisses and the feeling of skin on skin. In retrospect, it could have been, but as A'tugwewinu lay beaten and bruised, hands tied behind her back, on the floor of an Enforcers vehicle, she knew from that fateful day when the ones in power destroyed her village, that she would never again receive the gift of a serene morning.

The Enforcers had surrounded them, kicking them awake. Bèl sprung to action, going for the machete they slept on, but it was futile; instead they received a busted lip and cracked ribs for their efforts.

"I'll find you!" they screamed, struggling, as four Enforcers held them down, while two others had A'tugwewinu pinned with a heavy boot on her neck, harshly tying her hands. "I'll get you back, Winu! I'll—"

A shot rang out. Silence followed.

A'tugwewinu craned her neck as far as she could but all she saw was the crumpled form of her lover, lying there, unmoving. Tears threatened to spill over as a deep well of sadness overtook her, but for one small moment, as suddenly an overwhelming sea of fury took its place, digging its hooks into her soul. Her gaze hardened; her resolve completed. Whatever else she would do, she would resist until the end.

She stared down at the blood pooling around Bèl's body until the last possible second, as the Enforcers dragged her out and threw her onto the cold floor of their vehicle.

For hours the vehicle drove. They arrived at a large, outdoor enclosure with gates, barbed wire, and bars as far as the eye could see. The Enforcers dragged her out of the vehicle, opened the first gate, then another and another—the loud clang of each slamming shut behind them reverberated into her bones. Finally, they threw her to the ground, leaving her shackled, and left.

SHE DIDN'T KNOW *for how many days she walked from her village. Her feet were crusted from blisters and cuts, her shoes keeping more dirt in than out. When she first arrived at the concrete city, she thought maybe someone would have a pair of shoes for her, but she soon realized that these people, these countless numbers of people, were very different than those she knew in her village. No one cared that she looked like she was on the verge of death; no one cared that she was filthy and hungry.*

At first, she tried to find someone who knew about her village but no one had time for a hungry child pestering them for information or food.

She didn't know how much time went by, but she grew as the ribbon shirt lifted on her hip bones, where before it carefully nestled them. She stole and lied, and with every passing day she felt further and further away from her people, her village, her core. The connection between the spirits was waning. Except for the ever-looming shadow of death's gangly forms in the dark corners of the city. She saw him everywhere. Mocking her as she shivered to sleep, taunting her as she attempted to swallow, yet no spit resided in her mouth. Death was her only friend, as she grew lonelier in a city filled with more people than she knew existed.

In her most desperate hour, a shadow materialized over her. Thinking it was only death coming to claim her, A'tugwewinu ignored the presence. Finally, fingers softly pulled on the tattered remains of her once glorious shirt. She begrudgingly opened her eyes and peered into the most beautiful face she had ever seen. The figure crouched down. "I'm Bèl," said the melodious voice of the angel crouched before her.

A'tugwewinu sat up straighter. "Winu," she responded. Bèl nodded, then stood up and gracefully looked back at her, then beckoned A'tugwewinu forward. She struggled to rise, finally she followed behind this elusive person, tailing after them like a starving man, which in a sense, she was. Bèl was familiar in a way that was confusing, had she met them before? Had she dreamed of those eyes like onyx? Dreamed of that voice?

A'tugwewinu pondered the ever-brightening tether between her and this stranger, as they skulked through the shadows of the maze of streets that made up the concrete city. Finally, under a box and into a cloaked crack in a wall, A'tugwewinu came into a small room filled with cushions and random objects, a dwelling perhaps, or gathering of things utterly useless. Either way, Bèl opened their arms wide and said, "Welcome home" in the same tone her Kokomis would use when she would visit him.

It made tears well up in her eyes. She felt strong hands caress her skin as a whispered song and her sobs lulled her to sleep.

IT TOOK HOURS, but ever so slowly, the ties loosened, warm red lubricating the way. A'tugwewinu, finally freed, sat and held her knees close to her body. She peered around her and spied cages everywhere. Eyes were staring back at her. The stench of stale sweat and blood was permeating the air. She laid down on her back and inhaled deeply, letting the smell take over her feelings and her body. She closed her eyes and prayed.

"There was a time when îhkwewak were honoured. Every village had îhkwewak, they were needed to be the in-between for the spirits and the rest of us here in the physical world. Without îhkwewak being the bridge, we would be in the dark about so much happening around us. We would be out of balance with the world."

"How do I to talk to spirits, as îhkwew, Kokomis?"

The elder smiled, his dark wrinkled face lighting up in the presence of his small grandchild.

"You need to be very still, and very silent, oshis, then send your intent, kindly ask them for a message, offer them a gift for their aid, and they will come."

The old man picked up his grandchild and gently sat her on his knee.

"I am îhkwew just like you, oshis. In a few years when you receive your first marks, you will come to me and learn how to carry your role for our village."

Grandchild held grandmother, the smell of sage and sema, feeling of safety and kindred souls cloistered around the two.

"I can't wait, Kokomis."

A'TUGWEWINU LOOKED AT HER WRIST, blood wrapped around it like a bracelet, skin rubbed raw from the ties. She gently swiped at the blood, dragging as much as she could onto her fingertips. Three deeps breaths. Eyes closed. Focus on the intent. Slamming her hand down on the ground next to her, she called for them. "Giibi. I have nothing to offer you but this, please accept my blood as offering and aid me," she whispered. Her veins turned black, blood suddenly pouring from her wrists, saturating the earth around her. A moment passed. The bleeding stopped. The earth heaved and sighed, it trembled slightly. Wisps rose around her. Shapes in smoke winded around her body, tickling her soul.

Upside-down and backward faces greeted her, antlers and horns, hoof and claw all spoke to her. The rocks under her warmed. The dirt cooled. Her ancestors came, whispering soothing encouragement in ancient tongues. Reminded her they were always there.

What could have been hours or seconds went by. The smoke receded, the shapes dissipated, and the acrid smell and sound of screams, interspersed with eerie silence, returned.

A'tugwewinu opened her eyes, resolve set in her mind, the time for listening was over. All around her, physical beings approached, the call of the spirits bringing them closer, fear and trepidation apparent in their demeanor.

An old one crouched near her. "Who—who are you?" he muttered feebly.

"I am A'tugwewinu, last of the Andwànikàdjigan," she responded softly.

For a long minute, nothing happened. "Is it true?" someone asked, "are you really one of the marked ones?"

A'tugwewinu nodded and removed her over cloak, baring her arms and torso, neck and back exposed, every inch of skin covered in little red symbols. The shapes foreign to everyone. She sat down and everyone followed. She peered at the dozen or so who had approached her.

"How do you mark yourselves?" one asked.

"We don't," she responded. "When someone shares a story and we listen, the marks appear, and then, when we press it, we can, in turn, share that exact story word for word." She peered around her, the strangers' faces were dumbfounded. "Would you like to see?" she asked.

Several nodded. A'tugwewinu took a deep breath and reached for the markings near her right shoulder. She pressed it and words came out of her.

"In the beginning, God created the heaven and the earth—"

TIME SEEMED ENDLESS, yet patience eternal reigned inside A'tugwewinu. Some beings stayed simply to listen, having nothing else to do, others felt a calling and dedicated themselves to memorizing every word. Others yet felt the need to ask questions and pose opinions.

Taking a deep breath, A'tugwewinu felt emotion roll within her as she touched the marking above her left breast, the first marking she ever received. It was the last of the creation stories which she carried that she had yet to share. The most sacred story she carried.

"Before there was time, there existed the Creator, who slept at great peace within the silent vacuum of space—"

"—the Creator was awoken suddenly by a great vision; in this vision she saw stars and planets, a beautiful world called Earth, within it were great rivers and oceans, four-legged, winged, crawlers, medicines and plants of all kinds. Finally, after everything, in her vision she saw the two-legged young beings that would need to learn from everything that came before them in order to survive."

A'tugwewinu was restless, partially listening to the elder, but mostly staring at her breast, waiting desperately to see the marking that would appear there. She was so excited to have been allowed to attend the adulthood ritual of those born before her. She would have hers next year, but Kokomis said she needed to get her marks now in order to begin doing îhkwewak work. Her knees bounced up and down with untethered energy. The elder smiled as they completed the story. A'tugwewinu gasped as a sudden warmth pooled above her left breast and there rose up small red markings no larger than the length of her smallest finger. She jumped up and ran toward her mother and Kokomis, embracing them both as they congratulated her on her first mark.

A'tugwewinu was honoured that the village council had permitted her to get her first markings before her adulthood ceremony. Kokomis *told her that it was only because she was the only other îhkwew in the village and she had a lot to learn from him.*

The trio quietly removed themselves from the throng of celebrating families. They approached a withering stump on the outskirts of the village, one of the last remaining things that sometimes turned green, but otherwise remained brown. Kokomis rested his hand upon it and muttered a prayer. With his other hand, he grasped A'tugwewinu's small brown fingers and placed her hand atop his withering and callused tan hand.

A'tugwewinu gasped as the stump pulsed. A beat, unlike the one in her chest, but resonating nonetheless. Whispers filled her mind. Stories and poems from ancestors who looked through her eyes into this discarded landscape and wept for the mother they had lost.

Kokomis removed his hand, and with it, hers fell limply at her side. He gently reached over and wiped the tears from her face.

"Remember that the spirits will always be there, and that they will share with you the most sacred of stories," he whispered reverently.

When the Enforcers arrived to toss rancid food at them, they would pause from stories. When they grew too weary, they would retire. This left A'tugwewinu alone to ponder her reality, the losses she had been subjected to.

She lay restless on the dirt, staring at the darkened patch of dried blood. A deep ache of longing struck her heart. The anguish of being alone made her cry out, a deep bellowed scream pierced her throat. No more would gentle, large hands soothe her ills, or a sultry voice whisper tender things in her ear. No more would she have a heart to come home to. The name of her life's love spilled forth over and over and over again. Her breath ragged, sobs uncontrollable, the darkness of the night caressed her and offered comfort.

A jagged piece of the cage caught her eye. She sobered and resolved to have one last ceremony for her dearly departed.

"WHY MAMA CRYIN'?" *asked the small child.*

Kokomis picked her up gently and rested her in his arms. "Because your papa died, she is sad he's gone," he replied gently.

"No! Papa's right 'der!" the child stated, pointing to the shadow enveloping her mother in an embrace.

Kokomis sighed. "That is your papa's spirit, only I can see him and you, oshis. No one else. Your papa's body died but his spirit stayed to say one last goodbye to you both."

"Papa's sayin' bye-bye?" A'tugwewinu asked.

"Yes, he can't stay here, he has to go and return to Creator."

"No! He can't! Papa!" The little one cried and cried as she wriggled free of Kokomis' arms and ran toward the shadow.

"Papa! Don't leave!" With a watery smile, the spirit crouched down and kissed the top of her forehead, then vanished. A'tugwewinu cried and cried. Beside her, her mother removed the machete she always carried as one of the village warriors. She grasped her long braid in her hand, and with a sharp tug, cut it off.

Her mother picked up her inconsolable child and held her tightly in her arms. A'tugwewinu grasped at the back of her mother's neck, feeling tiny prickles of short hair for the first time.

Her mother never let her hair grow afterward.

A'TUGWEWINU GRASPED THE BRAID she had grown from birth, passing it over and over and over the small sharp piece. Her white-knuckled hands cramped from the lengthy effort until finally the braid separated, hair falling jaggedly around her shoulders. She held the long braid on her lap, her mourning over. Never again would the name Bèl leave her lips. Their spirit would join the ancestors in the spirit world and be at peace. A'tugwewinu would join them very shortly. Hazy like a dream, the death spirit skulked near her, becoming clearer by the minute.

SHE STARED AT THE BRAID FOR DAYS. Running her fingers down the bumps, her fingers were caressed by the frigid tendrils of death's tattered form, looming over her.

Still she told stories.

TIME WENT BY IN A STRANGE SENSE. The prisoners had dedicated themselves to memorizing the stories she told. A new nation not of her village, not of marked ones, but of memorizers arose. They sat as she told the stories and repeated the words over and over again. An informal resistance was growing among the prison. One of whispered words from ancestors and spirits, one of listening ears and watery eyes.

Death became a corporeal form, the gangly limbs tickling her as she attempted to sleep. Not long, soon, very soon, she would join her beloved.

The dull orb in the sky began to go down. A'tugwewinu embraced her old friend, death.

Suddenly, her friend jerked away from her, and with a sad smile, he vanished.

Confused, A'tugwewinu looked to the horizon, where a crouched shape fiddled with the metal of the gates. Finally, with the tools in their hand, the metal gave way, and the figure stepped through the gate and hopped toward the metal enclosing her cell. The cloak was pulled back and eyes like onyx peered up at her, her angel returned.

A'tugwewinu dashed toward them, her fingers outstretched toward the figure. But she dared not touch, for her fingers would slip through smoke and not feel that smooth velvet skin. She inhaled a sob and withdrew her hand. Dark fingers grasped hers through the bars.

A'tugwewinu's eyes shot open. "How?" she whispered reverently. How was her beloved still here? She saw them die. She witnessed the blood leave their body.

"I begged those spirits of yours to allow me to be with you once again," Bèl whispered sincerely.

A'tugwewinu let the tears flow freely from her heart, and gasped as she brought her forehead to the bars, and in between the cracks, felt that skin that she dreamed about.

"And now that you have, will you leave me again?" she asked, hesitant, afraid that somehow this was a dream, or that death had taken her after all and this was simply the afterlife.

"Never," Bèl stated solemnly. A'tugwewinu pressed her face to the bars as her chapped lips met soft ones. Bèl kissed her like it was the first time and the last time they kissed, like soothing water caressing a parched throat. They kissed without care of the Enforcers, or pending doom, they kissed like the world was ending, but really, wasn't it already over, and perhaps within this kiss lay the new beginning?

They pulled away from each other, breaths ragged, a haze of lust and eternal love around them.

"Let me get you free," Bèl stated.

A'tugwewinu watched as they wrangled with tools until finally the bars loosened and were cut with enough room for her to slip through.

She rushed through and tackled her love to the earth, her arms enveloping Bèl as she giggled and felt joy erupt from her. She trailed her fingers to the spot where Bèl was shot, feeling gnarled skin and matted scars instead. She breathed a sigh of relief. Bèl grasped her chin.

"You cut your hair too soon, Winu."

She smiled. "I'll let it grow."

Bèl smiled back. "Your execution was announced to take place in a few hours. Lots of important people and Enforcers are here to witness the last storyteller die. We need to go."

A'tugwewinu nodded. Softly, she clacked her hand against the bars. Soon, the memorizers came, they noticed the hole, and the younger ones slipped out. The older ones stayed behind. "We will only slow you down," one said. "Besides, someone needs to stay to tell stories to the other prisoners," another whispered.

She nodded solemnly. She grasped Bèl's small pointed dagger and looked at the old one in front of her. "Do you trust me?" she asked. The old one nodded. She lifted the dagger to the skin above their left breast and carved marking symbols, small scratches that bled. The old one hissed in pain, yet remained still.

"This is the first marking we receive, give it to those who dedicate themselves to this path," she explained.

The old one nodded and whispered his thanks. She gave him the dagger. As they left swiftly, she looked behind her to witness the others giving each other the marks.

She smiled, the marked ones reborn.

"SINCE TIME IMMEMORIAL, *our people told our stories orally, we always listened when someone shared a story, and we always shared the stories we carried."*

A'tugwewinu sat upright and listened attentively to what Kokomis was saying.

"But there were other people in the world who didn't share stories the same way. They would use tools to record their stories and put them in objects, and people would learn the stories from those objects."

"Wouldn't they just get markings?" A'tugwewinu asked.

"No. They wouldn't. If they didn't take the time to learn the stories from objects, they would never learn them. And they didn't listen to each other, so they never learned to share either."

A'tugwewinu frowned. What strange people, she thought.

"Not so long ago, some people rose to power, and they realized that if they destroyed the objects, no one would be able to learn any-

thing, and they could hold all the power. So, they did just that, and all those people without their objects forgot all their stories."

A'tugwewinu was even more confused.

"Around the same time this happened, our people noticed markings appearing on our bodies. These markings were commonly found on the objects that the people in power had destroyed."

"What does that mean, Kokomis?" A'tugwewinu asked, alarmed.

"We're not quite sure, but the spirits have told me that our way of sharing stories can't stay within our people anymore; it's time to share this way of learning with others. Just as we have adapted a supernatural way of learning, we are therefore meant to adapt to a supernatural way of sharing."

DAYS WENT BY, person by person, the young ones departed into different directions, pledging to share the stories with anyone who would listen.

Finally, there but remained A'tugwewinu and Bèl. She peered into the eyes like onyx.

"I was hoping you would give me the honour of the mark, as I would also like to pledge myself to this role," Bèl asked.

A'tugwewinu nodded. With a practised hand, she deftly carved the marks into Bèl's skin above their left pectoral.

"I am no longer the last of the Andwànikàdjigan," she whispered.

Hand grasping hand, she marched on into the unknown world, ready for this new awakening of the people.

Off into the distance, she spied the shadow of Kokomis, raising his hand in reverent salute. She nodded toward the spirit as he turned and vanished.

ANDWÀNIKÀDJIGAN LEXICON

AUTHOR'S NOTE: This story has been a way for me to research the Indigenous languages of my people, the Algonquin or Anishinaabe and the Mi'kmaq or L'nu. As I am not a fluent speaker, the Anishinaabe and L'nu words used in this book would not have been possible without the help from the Algonquin Way Online Dictionary from the Algonquin people of Pikwakanagan First Nation and the online Mi'kmaq Dictionary from the Mi'kmaq people of Listuguj. Chi miigwetch and we'lalin for these incredible online resources. There are also words in Plains Cree, for which I would like to thank Jerry Saddleback, fluent Cree speaker and knowledge keeper who shared îhkwewak/îhkwew with me. This story also used words in French. I apologize if my research and my use of these words has been in any way oppressive or misrepresented.

ALGONQUIN/ANISHINAABEMOWIN

andwànikàdjigan (*uhn-dwah-nih-kah-djih-guhn*): record; to set down in writing or the like, as for the purpose of preserving evidence

oshis (*ah-shis*): grandchild

kokomis (*koo-kuh-miss*): grandmother

PLAINS CREE

îhkwewak (*ih-kwey-wuk*) plural; îhkwew (*ih-kwey-wo*) singular: two spirit, all-gendered person

MI'KMAQ/L'NU

a'tugwewinu (*ah-doo-gway-wee-noo*): storyteller

FRENCH

bèl (*bell*): beautiful

STORY
FOR A
BOTTLE

DARCIE LITTLE BADGER

D EAR BOTTLE FINDER,
Please deliver this letter to CC. They live with our parents on the western shores of New Houston. Our house sits on blue stilts and is surrounded by rose bushes. Mom used to keep them well trimmed and blooming. I hope she still does.

CC—

Sorry. I never meant to disappear.

Thing is, I made a mistake during your birthday party. It happened after lunch, when y'all were playing beach croquet. Remember how bad I was, always hitting the wooden ball too hard and launching it into the water? That embarrassed me so much, I pretended to need a bathroom break and scuttled to the far end of the cove. There, I was alone, except for a couple of gulls fighting over a dead crab. The isolation didn't make me nervous. Didn't surprise me, either, since that area is unpleasant, with sharp pebbles outnumbering fine grains of sand. Even though I was wearing shoes, I could feel points digging into the bottoms of my feet.

As I knelt to look for pretty shells between the rocks, I got distracted by an intense flash of light on the ocean, the sun reflecting off something silver bobbing in the shallows. Curious me decided to have a closer look. Nearby, granite boulders, remnants of a pre-collapse sea wall that had been torn apart and scattered by the sea, jutted from the land; some were above the high tide line, and others were halfway submerged in the water. I climbed onto the nearest boulder and jumped from rock to rock till I was several metres away from land, balanced on the peak of a snail-crusted rock that was almost totally underwater. From my lookout point, I recognized the silver object as a small boat. It was shaped like a double-wide canoe with a flat deck. I didn't see any sign of a human pilot, but there was a hatch on the deck that could have led to an inner area.

It bobbed closer, and its pointed head turned toward me like the needle of a compass. I heard the high-pitched voice of a child call in English, "Hello? Come here!"

I shouted back, "Do you need help?"

"Yes! Please, help me!"

I considered returning to the party and telling everyone about the boat. Remember that mistake I mentioned earlier? Yeah. I decided to handle the situation alone.

From my boulder perch, I leapt onto the flat stern of the boat; it didn't rock much, as if stabilized by an inner weight or mechanism. The hatch swung outward with a creak when I pulled on its lever. The voice called to me from inside the dark interior, "Help me!"

They sounded so desperate.

The boat was much deeper than I'd expected, as most of its volume was hidden underwater, like an iceberg. Did you learn about those? There used to be ice in the Atlantic.

A ladder led from the hatch to the bottom of the boat, but I didn't notice it (because canoes—even big ones—should be shallow-bellied) and crawled in headfirst. I fell at least two metres before hitting the hard metal floor with my shoulder. Could have been worse, but the impact smarted like a barbed thorn, and by the time I stopped cursing, the boat was already moving, vibrating with the hum of a quiet motor. I couldn't see anything. The hatch had slammed shut behind me, and there were no sources of light inside. By swinging my hands side to side, I found the first ladder rung and climbed until I felt the hatch lever. It was locked.

I beat my fists against that metal door and screamed for you, for Mom and Dad, and for all our cousins and uncles and aunts and grand-parents. I even screamed for your annoying friend Webster, since I knew he liked to swim and might hear my voice. When that didn't work, I crawled around the boat, searching in the darkness for the child who had called for me. There was no child, although I bumped into a console near the bow. I pressed every button or switch I could feel, at one point even turning something shaped like a steering wheel. Nothing stopped the boat or freed me from my imprisonment.

At that point, there was a crackle of static, the kind emitted by radios. Speakers over my head chided me in the same high-pitched voice that'd lured me aboard. "Stop messing around. If you break the ship, you'll get stranded and die in the middle of nowhere."

"I can't see," I said. "Let me out of this place!"

"The lights burned out," she replied, "but shuttle A-3 is otherwise in top shape. Don't worry. My city is nearby; just sit tight for a couple of hours."

"What city?" I asked. "Am I being abducted?"

"Absolutely not. You're being rescued."

"From what? My sibling's birthday party? Take me home *right now*."

"Why do you want to return to that? Humans aren't animals. You're meant for more than survival. You can be a vessel for millennia of culture: art, literature, science, leisure, hobbies, and joy."

"I don't know what that's supposed to mean," I said, "but when it comes to culture and joy, I'm good. Can I talk to an adult now? Please?"

"You are." The voice of my captor dropped in pitch, no longer a cutesy toddler-shrill.

That's when I screamed.

Hours later—just two hours, according to my captor, but it felt like a lot more—the hull encasing me shuddered once and then the motor shut off. With a click, the exit hatch popped open. The dim yellow light that spilled into my prison was artificial. When I climbed the ladder and peeked outside, I saw six gray walls and no sky—I was in some kind of landing bay. A glass-encased security camera overhead swiveled until its robotic eye looked down on my upturned face. There were no other signs of movement except for the gentle rocking. Everything swayed side to side. That's how I knew that the little canoe had taken me to a bigger ship: a city floating in the gulf.

"Hey!" I shouted. "Anyone here?"

The voice responded from hidden speakers in every wall; I felt like I was drowning in her frequency. "Don't worry," she said. "You're never alone anymore. What's your name?"

I lied because true names don't belong in the mouth of danger. "Mona Lisa. What's yours?"

"Olivia. Can you say Olivia?"

"Olivia."

"No. Not Ol*iv*ia. It's Olivia. Your accent is so weird."

Her accent was the weird one. She spoke like an old-timey person from the twenty-second century. I didn't talk back, though. At that moment, my only goal was escape. Unfortunately, it seemed like Olivia had complete control over the floating city. She unlocked a door that connected the landing bay to a white corridor. The walls were covered with continuous, thin, transparent screens. They resembled the touch-sensitive digital screen Instructor Lee used in math class. His screens were just a half-metre wide, though, big enough to show us what an isosceles triangle looks like but not large enough to swallow us whole. Olivia directed me through a series of corridors and doorways. Dim yellow ceiling lights lit the path and went dark the moment I passed by them. She gushed about the perks of the floating city: VR game rooms, saunas, movies projected on vast screens, and hundreds of cabins filled with the personal treasures of "the founders of New America."

"Did you say 'New America'?" I asked. "No way. When was this city launched?"

"Two hundred and three years ago," she said. "You missed our bicentennial."

That's when I understood: I'd been stolen away by a shuttle to the remnants of a doomsday city.

I learned about doomsday cities from friends, not in history class. To celebrate the first day of summer, Morgan, Jessie, Pete, and I were telling scary stories around a campfire, and Jessie went, "Hey, wanna hear something creepy?" You know that guy. He'll stretch the truth like taffy for attention. Guess that's why I used to assume doomsday cities were fake.

Well, a broken clock is right twice a day, and life is sometimes so weird, it doesn't need to be embellished by Jessie.

The story goes: centuries ago, people were more likely to prepare for the end of the world than attempt to save it. A group of rich folks decided to build floating cities and live in the middle of the ocean, far away from the land's troubles. Two cities were launched into the Atlantic. One sank and killed everyone on board. The other city—New America—disappeared.

Some claim that New America is still out there, hiding, dying. A few people remain alive, but their numbers aren't great enough to keep the city running. Others say that the city itself—which was equipped with advanced AI—is lonely.

"What happened to everyone?" I asked Olivia. "Are they all dead?" Two hundred years had passed, but the founders could have had descendants or been medical immortals, those old-timey people who invested fortunes in anti-aging therapies and tech.

"I'm still here," Olivia said.

"Where? All I've heard is your voice."

"The control centre." She was quiet for a couple of minutes—that was a long period of time for Olivia. "I'm the ship, Mona Lisa, which means I'm more intelligent than a human."

Under different circumstances, I might have laughed. Yeah, AI used to be different before the collapse, mimicking sentience so well, people would converse with their own phones. But Olivia had a personality. That meant the ship was more complex than any tech I'd known.

Human minds rarely did well in solitary confinement. What about human-like ship minds?

I stopped walking at a fork in the corridor. "Go right," Olivia said.

I hesitated because my internal compass screamed: you've been here before.

"Are you sure?" I asked.

"What did I just tell you, Mona Lisa? Obviously I'm sure."

I wanted to trust myself—there's a reason why Mom always makes me her navigator when we travel. But I've never had to navigate through a monotonous web of ship corridors. Why would Olivia send me in circles? At the time, I had no answer for that question.

So I continued walking.

In between directions, Olivia described the city rules. "If a door is locked, I *want* it locked to keep you safe. Our high-voltage security system doesn't know the difference between a Mona Lisa and an intruder. Got it?"

"Intruders? So we aren't the only two here?"

"I never said that. There are pirates on the sea and my deck cameras might malfunction. Which reminds me: you aren't allowed to go outside. That's also for your own safety. Stay in your bedroom between sundown and sun-up. Morning and afternoon are for chores and you can study after supper."

I asked, "What will I eat?" I'd been too frightened and vaguely nauseous on the shuttle to notice my empty belly, but hunger made every step feel like two.

"There's plenty of food," she promised.

"And water?" I asked.

"Of course." She laughed at me. "The founders didn't build a whole city without considering basic human necessities."

"Then why aren't they here anymore?"

For the second time that day, she did not answer my question. Instead, Olivia tersely said, "Up those stairs."

I soon entered a corridor that had evenly spaced doors along one wall. They were numbered from 2-01 to 2-15 with brass plates. Olivia said, "Yours is lucky seven!" And then, when I opened door 2-07, she added, "Welcome home."

My cabin had three rooms (bedroom, lounge, and bathroom) and was larger than our house. It resembled a history museum or time capsule. The furniture, a long brown sofa, metal coffee table, four-poster bed, and several cabinets, were fixed to the faux wood floor (I could tell it was faux because the grain patterns on the planks repeated over and over again, lacking the originality of a real sliced tree). The walls in the bedroom and lounge were bright white and coated with the same kind of screen I'd noticed in the hall. The bedroom closet was packed with musty dresses and narrow slippers. Cabinets contained empty glass bottles and a variety of little gadgets like binoculars and a music box filled with gold chains. I only peeked at that stuff, since it most likely belonged to a dead person and I felt like an intruder in a grave.

"Olivia, who used to live here?" I asked, but she was not in a mood to chat, and the door had locked behind me.

That's when it really sunk in that I was trapped in an artifact with a cruel streak. I ran to the nearest porthole and pressed my face against the cool glass. Didn't see any land. Just calm black water and a cloudy night sky. I wrestled the porthole open, ignoring its squeaking hinges, which were like nails on a chalkboard, and leaned out as far as I could (up to my shoulders; honestly, CC, if the window had been wider, I might have leapt into the Atlantic in a hopeless attempt to swim home, 'cause that's how fox-in-a-snare desperate I felt). I stood like that and stared at the vague horizon until the ocean wind twisted my hair into a waist-length knot of salty tangles.

Do you remember when Grandpa taught us how to build a fire with dry wood, the sun, and a magnifying glass? He made us promise that, unless it was absolutely necessary, we'd only light fires in stone pits on the beach where there'd always be enough water to drench the embers after we finished. Then, he told us about the year he witnessed the south burn. We were all taking a break from weeding his garden. You and me sitting in the shade of a mesquite tree and flicking ants off our toes, while Grandpa lounged on his hammock. As he rocked slowly side to side, he said, "I woke up in the middle of the night because my throat stung like I'd gargled a cup of wasps. My lungs ached worse. They were starving for a breath of air. I barely managed a puff on my inhaler. I went to the window and opened it, thinking that fresh air would help me breathe, but the stink of smoke just increased. There was no escape from it. The whole horizon was burning.

"We lost our house to the wildfire that night, but others lost much more. Do you know how the disaster started? Some guy popping fireworks in his yard after seven years of drought. You kids be better than that."

After that story, I had nightmares about opaque air that hardened like concrete in my lungs. I dreamt that the edge of the world was burning and nothing but ashes remained in the fire's wake. I'd wake up sweating through my quilt, wishing that Grandpa never taught us how to start a fire because nobody should have that kind of destructive power.

But you? You loved starting fires. That's the year we visited the cove every week so you could watch twigs burn. Then, Grandpa taught us how to use a flint to make sparks, and you built fires at night for warmth and to cook our food when we camped on the beach. I used to consider your fixation dangerous. I was wrong. You must have lit hundreds of fires on the cove. Thousands! And you never ever forgot to drench their embers with water.

That first night on the ship, I stayed awake for hours, searching for a light on the horizon. A light from your campfire. A beacon for your lost sister. I thought about you and everyone else on that cove. How you'd notice I was missing and search the beach for miles.

I never saw a light, but I knew it was somewhere and that knowledge stoked my hope.

It still does.

I didn't get any sleep that night. Not for lack of trying. The floating city was so large and steady, I barely felt the ocean undulate beneath my back, but it was still difficult to relax. I haven't had my own room since before you were born, and even then, Mom, Dad, and the grandparents were just a shout away.

The first morning on New America, the ocean resembled a smooth grey mirror that reflected nothing. Olivia's voice chirped, "Wake up! I hope that you slept well." At least she hadn't watched me not sleep all night.

"I didn't," I said, blearily gazing at the wall. It wasn't like Olivia had a face I could address. In those first few days, it was a struggle to carry on conversations with a disembodied voice. "Please take me home, or I'll die from insomnia. I miss my family too much. Isn't it your job to keep me alive?"

"Time will cure that troublesome homesickness," she said, still chipper—her tone offended me more than the content of her words. "Eat your breakfast."

Olivia had left a plate heaped with smoked fish and cherry tomatoes outside my cabin door. The true significance of that discovery didn't sink in until later. Although it seemed weird that the ship could prepare and deliver a plate of food without any help, I was more concerned with the origin of the food. "Where does this come from?" I asked, wondering if she had to visit land to collect rations.

"A garden without dirt," she said. "The founders modelled it after space station greenhouses."

From that day onward, I spent eight hours a day doing two types of work: ship maintenance and gardening in the vast greenhouse of New America. Olivia actually believed that one prisoner could keep an entire city running. With every light fixture I replaced, another three burned out. I guessed the floating city was impressive in its prime. Lit up by wall-to-wall digital screens, powered by hundreds of machines that used the wind, sun, and waves to generate energy. But Olivia had inactivated the screens to conserve energy, since half the generators were busted.

She needed that energy for her eyes, which followed my every movement, and her voice. It was difficult to know when Olivia would speak. Sometimes, I could work for hours without hearing a peep. Other times, she rambled about the drama and lives of the founders.

During my first week tending the greenhouse, as I clipped red romaine leaves from mature lettuce plants, Olivia asked, "Have you gardened before?"

"Yes," I said. "Why?"

"You have a green thumb."

I looked at my hands; as expected, neither of my thumbs were green.

"It's an idiom, Mona Lisa!" she said, laughing, as if I should know some obscure old phrase. "You're good with plants."

I didn't tell her about our grandparents' endemic garden and the springs and summers we spent weeding, planting, and tending plants under Grandpa's watchful eye. Remember how he'd lounge in his hammock and holler out questions? "How much water did you use today? More than yesterday? See any thrips? That many? Might need to do something about those leaf suckers!" He said it was important to observe the ways of a garden 'cause although plants might not be able to talk, they show us what they need. In the greenhouse, I counted the number of cherry tomatoes on each vine, noted the carrots, onions, and potatoes that had sprouted, and kept track of every seed I collected or planted.

It became clear that something was wrong.

So I asked Olivia whether I could borrow a notebook and pencils.

"There aren't any left," she said. "Once you've fixed generator three, I'll give you a personal tablet."

I didn't need all the functions of a tablet. I just wanted written verification that my mind could still keep track of a garden. The numbers weren't adding up. There'd be twenty tomatoes on one vine in the afternoon and just eighteen tomatoes on the same vine the next morning. But when I asked Olivia, "Are you sure we're alone?" she just laughed and went, "Don't be silly. You're the only girl on New America, Mona Lisa."

"Food is going missing," I said. "Somebody else is eating the vegetables at night."

"No," she said. "You're confused. You miscounted. Humans make mistakes."

"Not this time," I said. I'd been so careful.

"When you fix generator three," she promised, "and your tablet is fully charged, I'll send you all twelve hours of video from last night. Nobody was in the greenhouse. Will that make you feel better, Mona Lisa?"

My sense of reality teetered like a ship on rough waters. "No," I told her. "Never mind."

You know how Grandma always says, "Old folks live in their memories"? In that respect, I felt a lot like an old woman at sea. Every night, after Olivia locked me in my cabin, I sat at the window and remembered. Do you remember those board games we always played in the middle of the night, when Mom and Dad thought we were sleeping? We'd hide the wooden checkerboard under my pillow and the bag of stone pieces under yours. Then, after the night went quiet, you'd set up the game. That was always your job, 'cause your hands were steadier than mine, all the better to place twenty-four stone chips on a hard surface without waking the house. I'd provide the light source, holding my book lamp over the board. Half the challenge of midnight checkers was holding still for forty minutes, since quick movements sent tremors through our old spring mattress and scattered the checker pieces.

C, those games were so much fun, but the memories haunt me in the worst way. You always lost gracefully. Just shrugged and said, "Maybe next time." I'd feign dignity, like a gracious winner, but that was all an act. Did you ever wonder why, right when you started winning anything, my luck went through the roof? It was all too easy to steal or switch game pieces in the dimness, especially since you trusted me. I'm a board game cheater, a self-centred, dishonest cheater, and I deserve to play with rabbit dung instead of game pieces for the rest of my life. Now, all those wonderful memories are poisoned by my dishonesty. I'm so sorry, CC. You deserved those victories and the chance to feel good about yourself. You deserved to celebrate your fourteenth birthday properly. If I make it home, I promise to make amends.

Fortunately, I carry more good than bad memories. Remember how often people mistook us for twins when we were young? We'd pretend to be hero twins every time we did good deeds, like delivering water to an Elder, cataloguing the seeds and vegetables in the garden, or cleaning rubbish off the beach. Then, I had a growth spurt, and people stopped asking, "Are you twins?" Losing that visual shorthand of our tight relationship bothered us so much, we decided to try and build a time machine so I could jump forward two years and let you catch up to my age.

I didn't used to reminisce this much, since I was occupied with life in real time. But here's the thing: living ain't enjoyable without you, our family, and our friends. I even missed the goat-whispering woman who gave us fresh eggs when we fed her chickens. I wanted to go home, and the closest thing I had to home on that city were memories.

Throughout the chores, routines, and chatter, I never stopped thinking about escape, but it wasn't until week three that my planning became desperate. I guess the salted fish came from a dwindling stock because one morning, after I'd brushed my teeth and dressed in a loose white jumpsuit from the bedroom closet, Olivia said, "You shouldn't wear white today, Mona Lisa. It'll get stained. Find something dark. Go on."

I swapped the white jumpsuit for a long black dress. When she saw my choice, Olivia said, "How apt. A mourning dress."

She guided me to part of the ship I'd never visited before; it was a metallic octagonal room with silver tables protruding from two of the eight walls. There were hatches and red-stained drains and gutters embedded in the floor. The air smelled like salt and death.

A rack of knives hung to my left. All the blades were sharp and clean.

"We passed a school of tuna earlier," Olivia said. "I felt them with my sonar. Finally! You can eat the meat fresh! Go. Check the trap under the centre hatch."

In the middle of the room, a dark chute dove straight into the dark ocean. It resembled a well. I pulled a wire cage from the water. As I wrestled my catch into the light, the cage shuddered from the struggles of two muscular fish. Their glinting bodies drenched my face with seawater.

"Wonderful!" Olivia said. "Once they're tuckered out, I'll teach you how to bleed them."

The tuna were gasping. Big gulps that made their gills flare. At that moment, I thought about Grandpa and the night the south burned. I thought about his struggle to breathe, the pain in his lungs, and the people who suffocated in their own homes.

"Please don't make me kill them," I said.

Olivia just laughed. "It's easy. Pretend they're wiggling squash!"

"No," I said.

"I insist."

We went back and forth like that and the more I refused, the louder Olivia's voice became. At last, she boomed from every speaker in every wall, "You aren't leaving this room until they're dead."

My ears ringing, I took a bleeding knife from the wall. Although the tuna had stopped thrashing, they still gasped for air.

"You'll thank me during supper," Olivia said.

One side of the cage could be unfastened and removed. I pinched my finger on a hinge as I opened it. I barely noticed the pain, although the metal cut deep. Olivia started talking, saying something about holding them under the head and belly.

"How much meat is in an average tuna?" I asked. "And how many tuna are in the sea?"

While she was distracted with my questions, I returned the open cage to the water.

"You shouldn't have done that," Olivia said. "Really."

"But I did," I said.

"You did," she agreed.

Without another word, Olivia locked all the doors in the killing room and turned off the lights. She left me there until I felt like a dying fish, aching for the taste of water.

As I suffered through, I made plans in the darkness.

Eventually, Olivia asked, "Did you learn your lesson, Mona Lisa?" Her voice was subdued, almost meek.

I answered honestly, "Yes." Then waited in dreadful anticipation for her to force me to kill before I could escape. But instead, there was silence, and I soon wondered whether she'd abandoned me. Would I die in a dark room that smelled of brine and blood? "Olivia?" I asked. "Are you still there?"

"If survival were easy," she said, "we wouldn't be alone in New America."

The lights flicked on.

"You should be grateful," she said. "I had nobody to educate me, Mona Lisa. But you have me."

I could have defied her. Defended all the lessons Grandfather taught me and everything I'd learned from Instructor Lee, our parents, and you, CC. But I didn't. Because I'd learned my lesson, and things were going to be different.

I don't know how many days or weeks passed before Olivia trusted me enough to work on the upper deck. A freshwater tank was clogged.

"Drain the tank, unscrew the lid, climb inside, check the output, clear the obstruction, and then return below deck," Olivia said. "Don't dawdle. There may be pirates."

"There may be pirates?" I repeated.

"Always!"

She said *may* be. Which meant she couldn't see everything.

It was the chance I'd been waiting for.

Inside the city, Olivia delighted in confusing me; she sent me in circles until I didn't know north from south. That's why my internal compass complained so often. When I stepped onto the sunny deck, my sense of space returned. I felt like myself again.

The moment my pupils adjusted to daylight, I scanned the deck for a suitable hiding spot, ignoring the large water tank in to my immediate left. Beyond an expanse of metal tables and chairs, there was a shed-shaped structure on the far end of an empty pool. Olivia chirped from the tablet at my hip, "Do you see the cistern?"

I tilted the tablet camera to the ground and pointed at the ocean. "Is it that?"

"Mona Lisa," she said, "describe *that* to me. The tank is big and shaped like a ten-foot-tall barrel."

She really couldn't see me. Dropping my tablet, I sprinted, leapt over a bent railing and landed with a *thunk* on top of a metal table.

"What was that?" she asked. "What are you doing?"

None of your business, I thought. As I ran, my antique dress flapped in the breeze for the first time in centuries, no doubt. It was exhilarating.

Then, Olivia's voice surrounded me, crackling from failing speakers throughout the deck. "You're being stupid! The pirates will eat you! Where did you go?"

That's when I heard a loud, electrical cracking, the same sound a stun gun makes. A tendril of light singed the air to my right. I had a vivid flashback to my ex's fifteenth birthday. You weren't there, but

Morgan hung a rabbit-shaped piñata from the mesquite tree in her yard, grabbed a wooden lacrosse stick, put on a blindfold, spun 'round until she staggered, and then swung wildly at the air, trying to split that rabbit open. I'd been standing to Morgan's right, near enough to catch her if she fell. The first swing had whooshed past my ear, sending a warning breeze across my cheek. I'd shouted, "Morgan, stop!" but all the other partiers were screeching, drowning out my voice. I dodged a second swing and threw myself to the ground. With a thunk, the papier-mâché head went flying, and the rabbit bled candy onto my face.

I prayed that Olivia would be less lucky than Morgan. My pace lengthened into long bounds. I was afraid that if my feet touched the deck, I'd transform into a lightning rod. With a final leap, I threw myself into the shed and slammed its door shut.

The shed, which contained a variety of cleaning implements, was large enough that I did not feel claustrophobic. I heard a couple more ominous stun gun crackles, but Olivia gave up quickly, likely worried about draining the ship's power.

After enough silence had passed to ease my anxiety, I cracked the door open and observed the water tank with the binoculars I'd carried from my cabin. There had to be another person on the ship, which meant the obstruction would eventually be cleared.

Night came. Behind me, a light sputtered awake, casting eerie shadows down the deck. Under my watch, a slender, pale figure dressed in white emerged from the hatch. Her shaved head was covered by a wire mesh cap, the kind that connects brain impulses to electronic devices. Although her face—long, smooth, white, and without freckles or pimples—could have belonged to a twenty-year-old woman, other parts of her body hinted at a greater age. Her neck was a stack of lovely horizontal creases, like rings in a tree. Once she had drained all the water and climbed inside the tank, I left my hiding spot, crept through the maze of fallen chairs, climbed the ladder on the side of the tank, and slammed the heavy lid shut over her.

That was a satisfying clang.

"Mona Lisa," Olivia said. I could barely hear her voice through the metal walls. "Why?"

"Somebody was eating my vegetables. Just had to be sure it was you. Take me home now. Real home."

Silence. And then she told me, in the smallest, saddest tone, "Before I was born, generations had names, but nobody bothered to name mine. We weren't expected to survive the hell we were born into. I've been alive for two hundred and seventeen years. Do you really think I conquered the apocalypse by luck?"

"There was no apocalypse," I said.

She opened her mouth, as if to speak. I didn't let her.

"Set a course to home," I said, "or I'll burn your city down, Olivia, and there won't be enough water in the ocean to save New America."

I wish you'd heard me, CC. I was terrified, but my voice didn't quake like it does when I give speeches.

That's when the city began to hum. I heard the familiar chug of engines and felt a breeze against my face. We were moving.

I still wonder what I would have done if Olivia had refused.

For the past seventy-six hours, I've been stuck on deck, guarding my former captor. She isn't allowed to go into the city. Too risky. We might not have food, but there's plenty of water, and New America will reach land any moment now.

I hope.

The sky is so beautiful tonight. Do you remember how we'd look at the stars, name our own constellations, and invent their stories? My favourites were dog and stick, one always chasing the other. And the swing made of stars. I said we'd fly up there someday, and I'd give you a big push, and you'd swing across the galaxy. I can see them now. All of them.

There's a pinprick of light on the horizon. A fire burning on a distant beach. Is it yours, CC?

It must be.

Love,

Your Big Twin Sister

SEED CHILDREN

MARI KURISATO

THE GIRL COLLAPSED AGAINST THE WHITE STONE WALL, sliding to the uneven marble floor in a slick whisper of her own darkened scarlet. She laughed, coughing up hot blood. It slipped from her mouth in rivulets as she spoke.

"It appears," she said quietly, "that I am dying. I suppose I should take a moment while I bleed out to regale you with how I got here, huh? Someone should know, at least." She laughed, spat blood, and stared at her audience a moment before beginning.

THOUGH THE STAR CALLED SOL once provided light for life on Earth for over four billion years, it was now a red rose of death, pouring heat and radiation throughout the solar system like a bright boiling blistering eye of disapproving judgment. Intergalactic blue fire spilling from the mysterious Ghost Gate had crashed into the sun, accelerating the sun's expansion and eventual death, increasing the star's size while sending its temperature soaring.

Unlike the Saturn Jump Gate, which had been discovered orbiting the planet Titan, no test pilot activated the Ghost Jump Gate that orbited the sun. No one knew where the Ghost Jump Gate even came from in the first place. The blue fire poured into the sun for three years and only ended when the gate itself broke apart, being swallowed by the now much larger sun.

The increased heat of the dying star scorched the earth, boiled the seas, turned vast tracts of farmland into dunes. Dust storms buried cities. Heavy winds brought skyscrapers crashing down. Man-made diseases on the continents struck down millions. Billions more sought to leave the planet before the planet burned, or before the weaponized plagues got them.

Those who could took orbital shuttles, or Seed Ships, that exploded from the earth like massive mountains of granite. As they rode magnetic waves of fire, they eyed the moon as a staging base or headed toward the Mars colonies. Others left for Ganymede, the outer solar system colonies, or the Titan Jump Gate Ring, risking death to traverse the great void in an instant on a one-way trip into the unknown.

Too many were left behind, too poor or too unskilled to secure passage off the Withering Earth, as it came to be called. Food and water became resources prized more than human life as millions of people died. One Seed Ship, hastily constructed from the cheapest nanomaterials available, broke apart as it rose into the sky, killing many on the ground and everyone within the doomed vessel. Few mourned those lost, as temperatures and food shortages caused worldwide clashes, and forced many to become cannibals just to survive.

Roving bands of humans fell back on ancient tribalistic bonds, twisting those laws into "kill or be killed." In more temperate zones, where food was easier to produce and more plentiful, those in power offered their citizens a grim balm: three years in a virtual paradise before being gently euthanized and being reprocessed into nutrients for other citizens. This proposition wasn't mandatory, and in areas where food was easier to obtain, not everyone took the offer, but for those who didn't work was hard and healthy cheap food was rare. Laws, such as they were, were strict.

For many, however, it was a better prospect than risking the lawless zones where the strong preyed on the weak—in many cases literally. Still, scientists in hardened hidden fortresses worked together, pooling their efforts and research with others like them to develop and mass-produce artificial means of extracting carbon dioxide from the atmosphere and storing it in vast blocks of concrete. They did so in hopes of lowering the temperature enough to buy more time for folks to develop alternate ways of surviving on the planet, either to reverse the course of catastrophic climate change or to leave the earth altogether.

It proved to be too little, too late. Even with surviving nations focusing solely on this technology, events had transpired to create a runaway climate change greenhouse effect on Earth. Despite the desperate efforts of the brightest scientists across the entire solar system, the rising temperatures caused by hundreds of years of human industrial waste heating the planet in combination with the massive heat influx created by the unexpected accelerated expansion and death of the sun proved to be an irreversible challenge. Advances were made every year in an effort to slow down rising temperatures, but it was only a matter of time.

Priority was eventually given to creating habitable worlds away from the Withering Earth; despite their invaluable contributions, synthetic citizens were barred from being allowed to escape with humans.

"AND THAT, MY DEAR LISTENER, IS WHERE I CAME IN," said the girl, smiling despite struggling for every breath. "You see, by my nature," she coughed, grimacing, "I had a problem with that policy.

"It wasn't just because I was the recreated mind of an Anishinaabe scientist, housed in an artificial body that had no 'human' flesh at all.

Nor was it because I was transgender, or niizh manidoowag, a carrier of sacred healing medicines of the Anishinaabe peoples.

"But it was that there are still babies amongst our kind, both Two-Spirit and not, amongst the humans, those who we called Children of the Light. Children who deserved better, but were ignored because of their artificiality.

"The Seven Teachings of my people insist that I live humbly and respectfully, but when our people's rights are ignored because we do not have authentic human flesh or authentic human blood, even though we bleed, I must abide by the teaching demanding me to be courageous and truthful.

"I have to fight for these children, because I am an Anishinaabekwe, an Anishinaabe woman who loves all her people, regardless of whether or not we were born in the wombs of our human parents or in the birthing crèches of the synthetic consciousness factories built and left to us so long ago.

"And so I fight to protect them. Regardless if they are authentic human or synthbabies built in crèches. They are all as equally human as me.

"It occurs to me that I should have brought body armour to this fight.

"I think I may pass out a bit just now.

"Sorry about that, dear listener."

THE GIRL GRUNTED AWAKE AFTER AWHILE. She sighed, looking down at her wounds, putting her hands over them. She forgot her silent listener as she pulled vials of mediflesh out of her rucksack and pushed them into the bullet holes, the white foam dissolving the glass and creating white hexagons of artificial skin and painkillers. It wasn't body armour but it should stop the bleeding, and maybe let her live long enough to finish her story.

She hissed as the mediflesh worked to repair the worst of her injuries. The painkiller helped but there was still a sheen of agony just beneath that. After a moment's sharp pain her vision cleared and she felt a little better. Less muggy and out of focus. She looked over at her "listener"—a tired-looking, ancient service bot with a single glowing green eye, indicating a powered-down battery.

"Ha," Nona said. "Get me a bit battle addled and I'm telling my life's story to a vacuum cleaner."

She wished she had a gun. Or a whole battalion. Or even just some soldier training beyond what she'd learned the hard way. She was outnumbered and definitely outgunned.

No playing around, Nona. A lot of innocent children were waiting on her to get them safely off the planet before the inhospitable environment destroyed their fragile bodies.

This left her with a hard choice. Her body was functionally organic but not made from human or animal flesh. As such, she had an option which meant she could save the children, but at a terrible price. She could forcibly activate her nanomachine abilities and harden her body, while speeding up her reaction time to speeds inhumanly fast. This would give her a tactical combat advantage, but it would mean something horrible. She wouldn't be able to stop herself from killing those who opposed her; something that felt sickeningly wrong, even though they were happily willing to murder her.

If she'd had combat training software, or combat experience as a trained soldier, she might be able to disable her opponents non-lethally. But she wasn't a surgeon with a scalpel, just a girl with a sledgehammer. In her enhanced mode, she had no way to make adroit attacks, just fast, efficient, and deadly blows.

Also, if she stayed inside her sped-up metabolic state too long, she would burn out her neural connections and end up brain-damaged or dead from overexertion. After all, she'd just been given a regular synth-person's body, not one built to be a combat tank.

But if she didn't act soon the people who were trying to kill her and the other children would destroy the Tree, their only safe way off planet. Then they *would* kill her, and then slaughter the children as "artificial abominations against God."

She bit her lip hard and leaned against the wall.

"The courage to be Anishinaabekwe," she whispered. Then she pushed off the wall, grabbed the service bot roughly, and stepped outside, her heart rate increasing as her skin began to harden.

It was a massacre.

THE ENEMY HAD MACHINE GUNS and railgun dart weapons, but they were only human, and accelerated as she was, she had the reaction times of a machine. She threw a service bot at one of the men, instantly turning him into paste. Nona punched holes through skulls, snapped arms like twigs, ripped people in half. Of the thirty sent against her, in the end only two remained, one human being who was too scared to fight her and a cyborg-enhanced fighter who matched her strength.

"You're a murderer!" the cyborg said, swinging his axe at her face.

"Who started shooting at who first?" Nona yelled, ducking his blow just in time. "You wanted to kill all these children, innocent and helpless!"

"You're all just fucking godless machines!" the cyborg said, turning to swing his axe again.

"We're alive, we hurt, we feel, and we pray, just like you," she snarled. Nona caught his axe and wrenched it from his grasp, before cutting off one of his hands. He screamed, and covered his wound with his other hand.

"Do it," he hissed. "Murder me, you gods-damned killbot."

She raised the axe—and threw it away. Nona looked at his human ally. "Run, but call for help for him. We didn't want this bloodshed. Remember—you started this." The woman stared, frozen in fear.

"Run!" Nona yelled, clapping her hands. The human woman bolted like a rabbit.

The cyborg stared at Nona as she collapsed.

"Why? Why didn't you kill me?" he asked.

"I never wanted to hurt anyone," Nona said. Then she puked up water and bile. Shaking. She wished she could have washed the blood off but all she could do was wipe it off with some rags she found on one of the dead. She smeared more of it than she removed.

The walk back to the children's hiding place in the ruined school bus took a long time because both the fight and her previous wounds exhausted her, despite the meds she'd ingested. She stumbled over the sand. Carol, the only human child in her group, yelled. That brought all the children tumbling from the ruined bus with shouts of joy and concern. They raced to her side.

"Sister!"

"Nona!"

"Mommy!" said little Tamba, holding up pudgy arms, demanding Nona hold her. Nona grunted and picked up the synthtoddler, smiling at the girl's green and chrome skin and bright blue eyes. The baby nuzzled her, and she patted her back gently.

"Shh, shh, it's okay, Tambarina."

"You're hurt," Carol said. She was only twelve years old but she acted like Nona's big sister sometimes. "Tamba, give your mommy some space, she's hurt."

"Noooo!" the child wailed.

Nona bounced Tamba up and down gently. "It's fine. I treated my wounds. The blood isn't mine."

"Oh," said Carol quietly with a look.

"Come on, we have to hurry and get to the Tree before sundown. Everyone ready?" Nona yelled.

There was a chorus of affirmative cheers and within a few minutes the little group of thirteen was on the move. Slower than Nona would have liked but it couldn't be helped. They stopped once to use "the potty" and to eat snacks, but Nona and Carol kept the group going at a good pace.

THE MALE CYBORG was still there when the group of children came close to the base of the Tree. The cyborg just waved with his good hand when some of the children called to him. One of the brave kids escaped Carol's grip and ran to him, giving him water and a few ripe pears. Nona started forward in fear but the male cyborg just nodded and gave the girl a smile.

Nona shooed the girl away and approached the man. "Are you going to be okay?" she asked.

He grunted. "They really are babies, aren't they?"

She nodded. He sighed and waved her on. That was the last Nona saw of him.

They reached the base of the Great Tree, soaring into the heavens like an immense wimba tower made of silver and gold.

Remembering what her auntie told her about the Great Trees before she died, Nona touched one of the bulbs of glowing blue at its base. The bulb opened to reveal a great flower with a luminous blue gel on it. It smelled like limes. Or oranges. Or orange limes. Nona put her hand inside before smearing the gel on the trunk.

The trunk shivered and unravelled, showing an immense teardrop-shaped seed the size of a mansion house, which peeled open to reveal a warm yellow interior that smelled of sweet-fruit.

"Everyone in! Quick now!" Nona said. She wasn't really sure of what was going to happen next but the kids, young and curious, tumbled laughing into the large pod. Carol looked at Nona with worry in her brown Indian eyes and Nona smiled. "It's fine. Relax. Get in, quick!"

Nona's confidence was entirely faked, but Carol got in nonetheless.

Once everyone was in, Nona touched the wall with her gooey hand. The seed shivered again and vines dropped from the wall. *Straps?* Nona had everyone put themselves behind the vines, which pulled the kids back gently against the wall until they were secured.

Suddenly there was a huge hissing sound as the tree corkscrewed the seed upward into the sky with great pressure. Nona wanted to pass out with the spinning, but most of the kids, even Tamba, laughed as they soared higher into the atmosphere like a top.

After about five minutes gravity went away and the vines loosened, letting everyone experience microgravity for themselves. Kids flailed, bounced, laughed, and screamed with delight. Even Carol, ever the serious younger sister, giggled as she cartwheeled past Nona, who inhaled deeply, glad for the breathable air.

Now what? she asked herself.

AFTER AN HOUR, there was a loud bang, then a clanging noise, and a series of pops. Nona frowned and looked outward, where sparks flared up, readying herself to attack whatever was on the outside of the seed wall. There was a crashing sound that popped her ears, and then she was staring at a small woman, a synthperson like her, holding a blowtorch.

"Riley," the synthperson said, "It's a seed full of little kids!"

Nona balled up her fists.

The woman grinned and put her torch away. Then she held out a lollipop. "Hi, I'm Sam! Are you lot hungry?"

Nona exhaled with a sob, laughing.

Tamba launched herself at Sam, who caught the toddler with a laugh.

A huge blond man, another synthperson, floated into view. "Hi! I'm Riley. Welcome to the Rose Dawn, orbiting Earth one hundred kilometres up. We're glad you lot made it. We're a refugee ship for synthfolks. But we won't turn away a sympathetic human, or three!"

Carol smiled with relief.

"This is a very interesting, uh, ship seed thing you have," Sam said, bouncing Tamba in her arms.

"A real Seed Ship!" crowed Mikan, a five-year-old synthboy.

"Right!" Riley said with a smile.

Sam looked at Nona. "Are you hurt?"

Nona felt her stomach drop. She looked at the ground and shook her head. "There were bad men that wanted to hurt us. I stopped them. I didn't want to do this, but—"

"Hey, hey," said Sam. "It's all right. I understand. Why don't we get you cleaned up?"

Nona nodded. "Don't take the kids away," she said quietly.

Riley shook his head. "We won't. Families mean everything to us. We'll just get everyone settled in and fed, and uh, bathed." He wrinkled his nose and Carol blushed under her tan skin. "And make sure everything's copacetic."

Sam grinned and led everyone in from the massive cargo bay where the seed sat, shining. Nona brushed her hand on the seed and bowed her head in silent thanks to the Great Tree.

They were safe. Now the vast possibilities of space awaited them, and sixteen-year-old Nona vowed to be there for her family.

All of them.

NAMELESS

NAZBAH TOM

ENNIFER SAT AT HER DESK, her tailbone aching from sitting in her chair all day. She moved her head side to side slowly stretching her neck. She yawned and reached for her cup of coffee, but as she wrapped her fingers around the mug she felt how cold it was. She sighed, looked at her wristwatch, and put her fingers back on the keyboard.

This was her last note of the day. She had sat through eight clients today. Seven of them were regulars but her last was a new client referred to Jennifer from his probation officer. She looked over the letter sent with the client from the probation department.

"Mr Trujillo is required to attend ten counselling sessions with a focus on skills development and substance abuse. One missed session will result in immediate arrest and incarceration.

"Mr Trujillo's counsellor will be required to send in a final report at the end of ten sessions with an assessment of the client's participation, progress, and skills development."

Jennifer typed in a short note about her first session with him. She typed quickly and succinctly with the words of her supervisor in her mind: "Remember to note sessions with the knowledge that it might end up in court one day. You don't want to tell too much or too little—

just enough to remind you of what you worked on together. Keep it vague."

"Client presents with complex trauma symptoms attributed to childhood abuse in foster care system, current substance abuse, street involvement, and is currently unemployed. Writer used Assessment Form 103-B to assess client. Writer is building rapport and trust with client and will continue to do so. Client's next session is next Friday at 4:00 p.m. Writer will finish filling out Assessment Form 103-B."

She was able to leave thirty minutes after five, enough time to run an errand before making it home for the night.

K'É SAT AT *THEIR KITCHEN TABLE sipping on *their juniper tea and eating pinches of cornbread *they had baked that morning. The clean pine flavour mixed well with the sweet cornbread. K'é sat in front of the window facing west in *their hogan, an octagonal home with a twenty-five-foot radius. *They lived alone in a hogan built to maximize space in *their solitude and thoughts. A hanging wood-burning stove to warm the cold desert nights. A doorway facing east to greet the sunrise. A bookcase filled with books and plants. A small couch and coffee table to write *their daily journal. A small kitchen table to sit at and prepare for *their next session with *their mentor, Asdzáá Hashké.

Asdzáá Hashké was a firm but loving teacher. Her voice could be heard clearly over a good distance with its booming high tone. Her chastising was as loud and expressive as her warmth and care.

"Yadilah!" she would exclaim loudly when she was exasperated with her students, jarring the classroom.

"Yáah, shiawéé!" she would say when she was proud of her students, soothing them all with her quiet smile.

In their last session together, however, Asdzáá Hashké's teachings were more alarming and urgent. K'é knew Asdzáá Hashké was part of the second generation who survived near extinction during the last

World War. But sitting on the floor of Asdzáá Hashké's hogan, she finally described her experiences in detail.

Asdzáá Hashké searched K'é's face ensuring there was a place within *them to place each and every one of her words. "During the last World War, our Navajo ancestors hid deep inside the cliff walls of the reservation and in underground bunkers to escape the draft. Those who were forced to fight tried to make their way back home to ensure the safety of their families. Very few returned. They were captured at checkpoints, jailed, or placed back at the front lines. The war raged on and we survived invasions from China and Russia. Larger cities and towns already debilitated by economic depression and climate change were captured first, but rural areas took longer to canvass and control. Beyond the safety of our canyons, the rich died at the hands of rebel forces, crops failed, and mass extinction became a daily reality. It was complete chaos."

Rivers of tears filled Asdzáá Hashké's eyes as she described how, despite bombs dropped, despite millions killed, despite the chaos of this new world, soldiers returned home because of dreams they had had.

"I was at my post and drifted off," Asdzáá Hashké remembered as this soldier spoke many years ago. "They had us standing guard for twelve to sixteen hours at a time. The air was electric with fear. I dreamt that my grandma, speaking from Spirit world as she had passed years before, sat in front of me. I could reach out and touch her. Before she faded away, she told me, 'Go home. This is not the fight we need you for. Your family needs you.'"

And finally, "An auntie visited me in my dreams. She said to me, 'Our people will not survive. Our ways and traditions will not make it if you are not home to learn.' She showed me images on the surface of her palm of what was going to happen. It was so terrifying at first and I couldn't watch. Then she opened her other palm and showed me images of survivors, my children and grandchildren and their grandchildren. I left my post and hitchhiked all the way home."

Asdzáá Hashké sighed heavily and braced herself on K'é's shoulder as if the memory had been too much. "K'é. Look at me. I am old now. I have to reserve my energy for Travelling between worlds. This requires long hours and a lot of rest. I cannot do this alone. I have a strong feeling in my belly that you have been Travelling already." K'é gulped at the offer, as if standing at the edge of a great precipice.

Now in K'é's hogan, *they took a deep breath and finished writing in *their journal *their truth, as if signing a contract to *their heart, to the future of *their people: *"It is time to tell Asdzáá Hashké my dream."* Before K'é could change *their mind, *they packed some cornbread and headed to Adszáá Hashké's home.

EVERY MINUTE JENNIFER SPENT at work led up to this moment when she would come into her favourite corner store, Lucky Convenience. Jennifer stepped in through the sliding automatic doors and scanned the aisles quickly.

"We meet again," she whispered under her breath.

She knew the anatomy of this store like the back of her hand. Each aisle from front to back was assigned various items starting with automotive and seasonal supplies. Next aisle belonged to travel-size toothpaste, single-serve aspirin, and emergency sewing kits. The aisle after that was dedicated to chips, candy, and gum, followed by baked goods. A coffee stand with doughnuts stood before the refrigerated section of sodas, juices, milk, eggs, butter, beer, and wine.

Jennifer learned which beer had the highest alcohol content as well as the cheapest wine. Reds over whites.

The hot dogs turned on the hot iron rods. The Slurpee machine mixed reds and blues. The smell of diluted coffee wafted through the air. She needed a six-pack of beer and a bottle of wine. She weaved between other shoppers swiftly, made it to the cooler, and grabbed her favourite brand of dark ale: Newcastle. She held the beer close to her as she made her way to the wines on sale a couple of aisles down. She adjusted her bag on her shoulder, freed her hand, and reached up for a bottle of red wine. She made her way to the front and stood in line with her items.

The cool bottles of beer and warm wine bottle pressed against her like a familiar weight to her arms and hips. This part—the relentless lineup—felt like the last hurdle before she was to head home and settle in for the night. She imagined the sweet aftertaste of the Newcastle as she waited for her turn. This made her salivate and stomach knot up. A white woman in a pantsuit stepped up with her items and fumbled with her payment. As the cashier rang her up, Jennifer tapped the wine bottle with a finger, impatient that it was taking this long for her to get home with her drinks. She wanted nothing more than to check out and to forget about her day.

While Pantsuit Lady desperately scooped change that had fallen to the floor, Jennifer's thoughts wandered back to her meeting with her last client. She didn't like court-ordered sessions, not because of the clients, but because it was coercive in nature. Judges didn't really care about healing. They wanted reports to move this client along either back into jail, or, if they were feeling charitable, they would track them into a rehabilitation centre.

Jennifer forced a smile as the client entered the room. "Welcome to my office. I'm looking forward to working with you."

"Me too." He tried not to sound too enthusiastic, but she had the power to send him to jail, so he played nice. He smiled with his chapped lips but his dark brown eyes remained suspicious. His wiry facial stubble framed his mouth and faded down his chin. Classic patchy Native beard pattern. Jennifer reminded herself to give him an outreach hygiene kit which had a razor, travel-size shaving cream, toothbrush, toothpaste, and underarm deodorant. His thin frame was engulfed by the chair he sat in. He wore fitted jeans, a canvas belt buckle from the Army surplus store on Valencia Street, a black T-shirt three sizes too big, and an old pair of red-and-white Jordans with shoelaces he had knotted where the lace had come apart. Jennifer watched him as he carefully scanned the room. A diploma. A large black filing cabinet. The computer turned away from him. A poster of the Seven Sacred Teachings. An abalone shell with a bundle of sage sticking out of it. The usual books about addiction and trauma. A cup of cold coffee in a brightly coloured Pendleton mug.

"Would you like some water or a snack?"

"Sure."

She handed him a granola bar from a box she had in her bottom desk drawer and a bottle of water.

"I keep some for clients in case they're hungry."

He opened the bottle of water and granola bar. The bar was gone in two bites. He washed it down with half the water in one gulp.

"I like granola bars too," she said. "Especially the ones with chocolate."

"It's all right. Thanks. So, what do we do now?"

"Well, we will work on an intake. It's a lot of questions, some of them can be difficult to answer. You can take your time or not answer any of them. Your choice. Cool?"

"Cool." They both knew he didn't have a choice. He had rehearsed this story so many times. He knew how to share without feeling any of it. No one really cared anyway. He wanted to stay out of jail and she was just meeting with another client.

"Okay, next." The cashier waved in Jennifer's direction. Jennifer shook her head and placed her purchases onto the conveyor belt, the image of the client's patchy beard still fresh in her mind.

K'É COULD SEE ASDZÁÁ HASHKÉ'S new hogan sitting in the desert's late afternoon sunlight. As *they approached her front gate *they noticed a small garden of corn, squash, and watermelon. K'é said a silent prayer over the seedlings in the hope that the soil would sustain the crop, twenty years after the war's destruction. K'é marvelled at the hogan's construction and rejoiced in Asdzáá Hashké finally living above ground. Many of her generation were finally emerging onto the landscape after two decades of surviving in connected networks of underground bunkers.

K'é could see through the front window that Asdzáá Hashké was waiting inside drinking tea. K'é knocked on the door.

"Shimá, you home?"

"Aoo', come inside."

K'é turned the metal doorknob, pushed the wooden door, and entered. Asdzáá Hashké was seated at her round kitchen table. The rich brown of the table had faded and there were four mismatched chairs around the table. She sat in the most comfortable one, wide with chrome finish and faded blue cloth cushion and back. There was an extra pillow on the seat. Beneath her to the left of her chair on the clay tile were grooves etched out from her whorl that danced and jumped against her leg when she spun wool. Her balls and skein of yarn sat in a basket on the small sofa behind her chair. K'é sat on the metal crate closest to her. Asdzáá Hashké poured tea from a metal kettle into two matching cups. K'é enjoyed the momentary silence as *they gathered *their energy and attention. As *they sat sipping from *their tea, Asdzáá Hashké finally spoke. K'é knew better than to speak before *their elder.

"You've learned a lot these past few years, yáázh. I'm proud of your progress. But part of progressing is owning your truth. Do you have something important to share with me today?" Asdzáá Hashké peered into the depths of K'é's face in a way that only a nádleeh or Medicine

Person could. K'é gulped, unsure if *they were brave enough to carry on these traditions.

"Sometimes, I dream. Sometimes, I swim with whales and dolphins. Other times, I am learning to fly. At first it's this awkward frog-legged movement that gets me a few feet into the air but soon I can frog-leg myself above the trees and see everything below me." K'é paused for a moment and looked at Asdzáá Hashké, wondering if *they sounded silly. Asdzáá Hashké nodded, encouraging the truth to come forth, knowing not all had been said.

"Now the dreams are getting stronger. More vivid. Last night I dreamt that I was helping out with some ceremony." K'é focused *their eyes so hard that wrinkles appeared on *their forehead.

I'm outside a hogan. It's a sunny day, blue skies forever. The land is dusty brown and there is a mountain behind me. I see homes that are boxy and painted different colors on the hill behind the hogan. There are a lot of people at this ceremony. I see people arriving in trucks and cars. Some have arrived on horses who take cover from the sun under trees nearby their tails swishing away flies as they lazily chew hay. Anyway, I'm standing outside this hogan. I see people who feel familiar but I don't recognize them.

K'é opened *their eyes and realized *their hands were intertwined with Asdzáá Hashké's, as if they had both been on a long journey, as if she needed to look through the window on K'é's memory.

"Shiyáázh," Asdzáá Hashké said, looking into K'é's eyes. "Everyone can dream. But it sounds like your dreams are asking you to do more than watch. They are asking you to Travel. To send a message to another the other side. Would you like to learn? Would you like me to teach you?"

"Yes, shimá."

JENNIFER'S USUAL SIX-PACK and bottle of wine had done the trick again and she was passed out on the couch watching *The Late Show*. Beyond the show's audience laughter and celebrity conversations, other voices began to echo between her ears. In her usual drunken stupor, she never dreamed. But, tonight, the sensations were inescapable.

It's dark and warm. There are hushed voices all around the room that Jennifer finds herself in. Her eyes slowly adjust. There's a smoke hole right in the centre of the room with a shaft of light pouring in. Dust hangs in the air, small particles that move like a school of fish with each exhale and brush of hand in the air. There is an entrance covered by fabric of some sort. Jennifer looks down and sees that she is shirtless. There is a bunch of green plants in one hand and a braid of plants tied around her other wrist. She sees her chest has been dusted with black paint. She looks down and sees a flattened chest rather than her breasts.

"Turn this way." A voice breaks the warm silence and Jennifer looks at a hand reaching out of the darkness to fasten the braid on her wrist. Another hand touches her on the back, adjusting a thin sash hanging from one shoulder to the opposite hip.

"TELL ME THE REST OF YOUR DREAM," said Asdzáá Hashké.

K'é continued.

I hear voices inside the hogan. Many voices. I look down and see that I'm wearing blue leggings, a shirt that is buttoned up, and shoes that feel tight. I have on a hat with a white brim. My left wrist has a beautiful black leather wrist guard embellished with a silver and turquoise pattern. It's my shield.

"Are they ready?" I say this to the folks inside the hogan although I don't know who I'm speaking to or about. After a moment, the voices inside say to me, "Aoo'." I lift the flap to the hogan and as my eyes adjust to the folks standing inside, I wake up.

SHE HEARS A DEEP VOICE *from outside the room. "Are they ready?"*

After one final adjustment of fabric around her head she hears the word, "Aoo'." Jennifer knows that word means "yes" yet she has never heard it before.

Jennifer woke up suddenly. She tipped her bottle of wine over and its contents soaked through the edge of her sofa. Her face was damp with sweat and her shirt was covered with the remnants of orange Cheese Balls. "Shit." She pulled herself up and rubbed the sleep from her eyes. She checked the clock on the wall. Six a.m.

She put the wine bottle on the coffee table, pulled herself up from the couch, and walked toward the bathroom. The warm hug that had her floating in a cloud of numbness all evening had been replaced by a sinister grip of the morning. She felt herself getting sick. With her hand on the wall, she found the toilet, dropped to her knees, and dry heaved. Snakes of saliva and vomit dangled from cracked lips. Her head reverberated with pain and she pulled herself to the sink and slowly washed her face. She cupped the cool water, sipped a little, swished it in her mouth, and spat it out. Her mouth tasted sour. Soon her face started to tingle and come alive. She could feel the cool tiles underneath her feet. She had two hours to make herself presentable for work.

As she sipped Pedialyte for breakfast and ate small bites of toast, she searched her wrist for the braid of plants. She stood frozen for a moment remembering small slivers of her dream. She looked at her kitchen with its bright overhead light littered with dead bugs and suddenly remembered her dream's dirt floor, warm darkness, smell of smoke, and soft voices. Jennifer looked down at her hands holding her toast. Her mouth went dry and her tongue moved gritty pieces of toast to the back of her throat. As she swallowed the toast, she realized she had swallowed too much and the pressure of the lump of toast moved down her esophagus painfully.

She touched her chest and felt the soft mounds of her breasts. Jennifer vaguely recalled the greasy black paint across the flat chest in her dream. She swatted crumbs off her chest, took one last sip of her Pedialyte, grabbed her bag and keys, and with a sigh, opened her front door. Jennifer leaned against the cool of the door with her forehead as she locked it and walked down the hallway toward the street. Hoping to not run into anyone she knew, she slipped on her shades, and made her way to work.

Once she got to her desk and opened up her email, she saw a reminder about Elder Thomas's visit.

FROM: Moves Camp, Leslie
TO: All Staff

Reminder that we are still taking one-on-one sessions with Elder Thomas who is visiting with our staff this week. He is here on Thursday afternoon and Friday afternoon 1:00 p.m.–5:00 p.m. Thursday afternoon he has 30-minute sessions with clients, so please make sure you help clients schedule time with him. Additionally, if staff would like a 30-minute time slot with him please let me know by the end of day today. Be sure to bring some tobacco to offer Elder Thomas. You are invited to the community feast Friday after work in the Great Conference Room here at the Indigenous Health Centre 6:00 p.m.–8:00 p.m. If you would like to volunteer to help set up and clean up, please let me know as well by the end of today.

Have a good day!
Leslie Moves Camp

JENNIFER EAGERLY SIGNED HERSELF UP for a consultation with Elder Thomas. She hoped he knew the word she heard in her dream. She wrote it down on a sticky note. *"Oo?! Sounds like oat."*

ASDZÁÁ HASHKÉ LISTENED INTENTLY. After hearing about *their dream, she knew K'é was the right choice as her apprentice. *They were already Travelling to the other side and visiting ancestors.

"Yáah, that's a beautiful dream." She twiddled her fingers in excitement. K'é sat looking at *their empty tea cup, waiting for Asdzáá Hashké to help *them make sense of *their dream.

"You made contact with our ancestors from long ago, shiyáázh. I was right in choosing you as my apprentice. Right now, you are Travelling by accident. But I can teach you to Travel there on purpose. Do you understand?"

K'é felt the hair on *their arms slowly rise. *Their vision sharpened and *their mouth became dry. *They took in this information nodding slowly. *They knew what this meant. "I'm a Traveller? Someone who can journey from this world to next?" *they asked in a mixture of excitement and fear.

"Aoo'. And, we must teach you how to handle this energy so we can communicate with our ancestors. I want to get some messages across." K'é nodded, took in a huge breath, and let it out slowly.

Asdzáá Hashké laughed. "Hey, it's not that scary. I've been Travelling for many decades now. We're going to do it together."

K'é looked up from *their tea and a smile formed on *their lips. Asdzáá Hashké got up and poured *them some more tea. She shared the cornbread K'é had brought. *They dipped their bread into *their tea and gathered *their thoughts. It was going to be an exciting evening.

After they finished the cornbread and tea, Asdzáá Hashké's face lit up.

"Okay, let's begin. Get comfortable in your chair. Ready?" She looked right into K'é's eyes with her eyebrows raised. K'é nodded and took in a deep breath. "Aoo'."

"The first thing we will do is slow everything down with our breath and attention." She slowly raised her hand from her lap to the height of her head with an in-breath and lowered her hand with an even slower out-breath. She did this for ten minutes, all the while K'é found *themselves getting sleepier and sleepier. "Try to stay in both the here and now and the dream world. That's the doorway."

With eyes half-closed and body half-present, K'é nodded *their head slowly and followed Asdzáá Hashké's hand rising and falling. As her hands slowed down even more, she started asking *them questions:

"Where are we now?"

"Ah ... sitting in a truck playing with some house keys ... or ..."

"Do you see me?"

"You're ... off to the left side of me ..."

"What am I wearing?"

K'é let *their eyes close to concentrate more. "You have on grey pants ... light brown or a cream-coloured shirt and a jacket ..."

"What else do you see?"

"The inside of the truck, the keys in my hand, and we're in front of a house ... it's blue and has white trim on the windows with flower boxes underneath the windows. I feel like I know the people in the house ... wait, the image is dissolving away ..."

"It's okay, stay with me ... I'll see you inside."

K'é's eyes fluttered open and for a split second saw Asdzáá Hashké with her hand on the table and her eyes rapidly darting back and forth beneath her eyelids, as if in a trance.

Asdzáá Hashké called K'é back into the dream and K'é followed by closing *their eyes. "Where are we now?"

"There's a sink to my left and your right. Why can't I see your face?"

"Try not to focus on that too much. I can feel you in the space ... focus on that sensing ... relax yourself a little more."

"Okay ... am I dreaming?"

"You're Travelling now. Keep going."

"I know we were just outside and now I'm here with you standing in front of me ... I still can't see your face but you have on the same clothes and you have to head out somewhere. Oh, this is so strange to tell you that I just dreamt about you while we are Travelling. I mean, we're Travelling together ... I'm following you ... uh ..."

"They're the same. The only difference is we know how to do this on purpose. I'm going to go now and you will wake up soon ..."

The image dissolved slowly. K'é took one more look out the window to the field of blue-grey sagebrush, red dirt, and mesa dotted with pine trees. The feathered clouds fell from the sky and K'é opened *their eyes to see Asdzáá Hashké looking at *them from across the table. She put her hand over *theirs and smiled wearily. "You did well, shiyáázh. Not bad for your first time following me in."

K'é returned the smile and noticed *their shirt was damp from sweat and *their hands were clammy. Asdzáá Hashké squeezed *their hand and then K'é pulled *their hands down to their pants to wipe *their palms.

"Wow, I'm tired," K'é said.

"Let's take a few minutes to recover before we go in again, okay?"

"Okay. Thanks." K'é sighed and got up to get a glass of water for both of them.

"That's the trade-off. You get used to it. I learned to not do anything too demanding after Travelling. You're young yet, so it won't be too tiring when you're starting out."

"It reminds me of those dreams I have where I fly around. I wake up feeling like I ran a marathon."

Asdzáá Hashké smiled. "It's one thing to figure that out on your own. It's another to bring someone in with you and lead them through."

"Will I learn how to do that too? To lead someone through?"

"Yes, but for the next while we will just have you follow me in."

"Where do we go when we go in? I know we call it dreams, but where are dreams?"

"We don't go anywhere; we're already there. We are using our mind and body to shorten the space between the worlds so we can enter—it's a shared space. Does that make sense?"

"Not really ... but I trust you."

"In our next jaunt in, stay close by. I need your energy to get a message across to a relative. Will you do that for me?" she asked behind tired eyes.

"Of course, anything you need."

"You see ... I'm too old now to do this on my own. I'm going to need your help. And you kind of owe me one," Asdzáá Hashké said jokingly.

"What do you mean?"

"You remember how I told you that people returned to the reservation because they were all being guided by dreams? And remember how we all hid in our canyons and bunkers and how it saved us from destruction? Well guess which old woman Travelled to your mother's dreams to make her return home?"

"Mine?"

"Yes. And guess who she was pregnant with when she finally arrived?"

"Me?"

"Exactly. Now it's your turn to Travel and dream our ancestors back to their rightful home."

"Whoa." K'é considered the enormity of this knowledge, like considering the enormity of the universe, all trapped in the body of this supposedly frail elder.

"I know. It's big. It's confusing," Asdzáá Hashké said with a chuckle.

K'é sat down in front of Asdzáá Hashké. Again, just like last time, she raised her hand and started the slow breathing. K'é closed *their eyes and slipped into the dream.

*They are on a couch. Asdzáá Hashké sits on the chair at the kitchen table nearby.

"Good, you made it through. I don't think our relative is here yet. Let's look around the house," she says as she stands up and walks into the kitchen. K'é looks around and notices how messy the room is. Cheese Balls littered across the coffee table. A bottle of Pedialyte, half empty, sits on the counter. A bright overhead light is littered with dead bugs. The sound of keys turning the lock. The front door opens. *They look up and notice a woman standing in the doorway. She looks back at K'é and Asdzáá Hashké in confusion.

"Oh god. Am I dreaming again? Wha ...? I think I fell asleep in front of the TV again. Where am I?" The woman motions to leave, panicked.

"No, stop! Don't go! I mean ..." The woman recognizes K'é's voice. She looks back and forth between K'é and Asdzáá Hashké in confusion and fear. K'é looks toward the kitchen at Asdzáá Hashké wondering what to do next.

"Hello, Jennifer," Asdzáá Hashké says calmly.

"How do you know my name?!"

"We were waiting for you. I'm just making my rounds visiting family."

"I don't understand. You're family?"

"Aoo', shiyáázh. Listen, K'é and I don't have much time. We have to go soon. So I need you to listen to me. You need to come home."

"You need me to what?!" Jennifer says incredulously.

"Come home. There's no more time for being lost. It's time to be found."

Jennifer watches the two visions disappear into the ether before hearing Asdzáá Hashké say one last time, "We have to go now. Come home, Jennifer."

ELOISE

DAVID A. ROBERTSON

CASSIE'S EYES FLUTTER OPEN and she can see a beam of sunlight crossing her room at a forty-five-degree angle from a rogue crack in her blackout blinds all the way to the pine baseboard that her bedroom carpet is tucked under. She stares at the beam and watches dust particles dance within it like embers around a campfire, like they hear music that nobody else can hear, like they know something beautiful that she does not.

She used to know, in a dream, but it's slipping away with each passing moment. She slides her hand out from underneath the sheets, places it against her cheek, and runs her fingertips across her skin like it might tell her what she knew once, what she knew seconds ago, like every translucent follicle of hair is a letter in braille. Then, she holds her hand out, washes it in the beam of light, and moves her fingers as though she's never seen them before, as though they're dancing with the particles of dust, like she can hear the music, like she can remember something beautiful.

Her skin is milky smooth and unblemished; it wasn't always this way. In the dream, sitting on the bed, smelling sterility and death, her skin was loose as though melting away, her veins thick with the brevity of life, and the lines, all those lines burrowed deep within her flesh. There was another hand: its fingers cross-hatched with hers, a shade of olive contrasted against her own pinkish white. It was a lovely pattern, Cassie's fingers locked within hers.

Emma's.

"You silly girl," Cassie says, repeating words, the only three words she can remember from the dream, like lyrics to the song the particles were dancing to, the song that nobody else can hear.

Silly of me, Cassie thinks, to keep dreaming of Emma, so many months after they'd met, so many months of waiting for Emma to call her, so many months of disappointment.

The dream is always the same, and this is the only reason why Cassie is able to remember anything about it. She has taken images from one night, others from a different night, and so on, and pieced them together like a jigsaw puzzle to form something of a memory, and then has, in turn, dissected the meaning of it.

"Why do I keep dreaming about her?" Cassie had asked her mother one morning, when the dream had become part of her routine. Like showering. Brushing her teeth. Dressing. Breathing.

"Does it matter?"

"Of course it matters."

"If she didn't call you, Cass, do you think she wants you to call her?"

"I was talking about the dream, Mom."

"Do you think she dreams about you?"

Cassie held the phone away from her ear for a moment and fought the urge to throw it against the wall. "We're always old. She's dying and I'm old and as soon as she dies, I wake up."

"What do you think that means?"

Cassie sighed. She had held her breath in until sighing, and now expelled all of it in one fell swoop. "That we're dead, and I should shut up."

"Maybe you were never anything."

Cassie hung up the phone, thinking that her meeting with Emma, though fleeting, had meant everything.

But now the moment is gone, and the echoes of it is haunting her while she sleeps. Echoes of a life that never happened, from a moment that did.

Why.

The radio turns on at precisely at eight a.m., Cassie's alarm clock. She is always awake before her alarm clock. Her dreams are her alarm clock. Her dreams are not timed well. Her dreams are entirely inconvenient. Cassie pushes herself up and sits at the side of her bed, her naked feet dangling close to the carpet, her toes brushing against the fabric. She reaches out with both hands, stops when her hands are awash in the shaft of light, cups them, then pulls them toward her body like she can bring the light with her, like she can wash her body in it: her eyes, her mouth, her hair, her heart. Like the sunbeam is smoke billowing from a smudge bowl.

She stops.

"Why did I do that?"

There is a piece in the jigsaw puzzle she created, that she continues to create, that looks like this. Pulling smoke toward her body, feathering smoke toward Emma.

The radio is on. There had been a song playing, but now it has ended, and commercials blare out of the speakers. These are the worst, a pet peeve on the level of missing socks. Radio commercials. A jingle about getting a vasectomy. Whatever song the dust particles are dancing to, this is not it. Cassie begins to thrust her fist downward, aiming squarely at the snooze button, but stops mid-air.

"Need an escape?" a man asks through the speakers of Cassie's alarm clock.

Her fist hovers in the air.

"Need more time?"

Cassie doesn't know what she needs. The radio cannot give her what she needs. The radio can't even wake her up in the morning.

"Do you have a problem child who needs some behaviour modification, but you just can't stand to send them away?"

"God no," Cassie says, then lowers her fist, hits the snooze button, and the radio stops asking what she needs.

In nine minutes, the radio will turn back on.

Cassie whips the blinds open as though tearing off a Band-Aid, light chases away the darkness, the sunbeam disappears in the crowd, and there is no more dancing, no more music.

There are eight minutes left.

She has a shower and just stands there, her head pelted by water from the massage setting of the shower head, her hands pressed against the fibreglass shower covering, her feet in a fighting stance, like she's trying to push the wall down. The heat is on high, and as water runs down her body, steam envelops her like smoke. Trying not to think about the dream makes her think about the dream. She straightens. Moves her hands to bring the steam toward her body, but snaps out of it and cleans herself in another way: brushes her teeth while in the shower. Shampoos and conditions her hair. Lathers and rinses her skin.

There are three minutes left.

She steps out of the shower and leaves wet footprints that lead from the shower to the mirror above the sink. She wipes steam from the mirror and stares at herself until she is only a blurred impression, steam stubbornly covering the mirror again. She wipes it away, it gathers again, she wipes it away, she sees herself old, sees herself young, over and over again. Thinks of Emma. Lying in bed, eyes closed, face turned toward the window, toward the sun. Cassie turned her head that way. They are old like that, like the reflection Cassie sees in the mirror. The steam is allowed to gather, until Cassie looks old again.

There is one minute left.

Cassie reaches forward, places her index finger against the silver glass, and runs her fingertip across the surface in perfect cursive, revealing only pieces of herself in delicate lines. An incomplete puzzle. When she is done, she takes a step back and reads her writing. *Silly girl.*

Nine minutes have passed.

The radio turns on, as though it was never off, announcing its presence in mid-sentence.

"—you disabled, and want to live with all your faculties for a lifetime? Jump out of that wheelchair and run a marathon? Ten marathons? Run across the world? Do you want to learn how to accept your disability?"

Cassie hears the radio and rolls her eyes. The commercial plays incessantly, like a Beyoncé or Taylor Swift or Drake song. "Then you've gotta try The Gate," she says with a large measure of sarcasm, "and never leave your home again." She looks away from the words on the mirror, even as they are devoured by the steam, opens the door, enters her bedroom, and walks purposefully toward the radio.

"Have a lost love that you just want a second chance with? Don't take it from me, listen to the words from Subject Zero, the original Gate participant."

Cassie stands in the middle of the room. Stares at the radio. She hasn't heard this part before. This part is not like a pop song.

"Hi," a girl's voice says, and Cassie flinches in disbelief, *"I met someone and let them go—"*

Cassie rushes to the radio and picks it up. Cradles it in her palms with such care, like it might crumble into dust just by breathing on it. She is breathless.

"—but with help from The Gate, I was able to spend my last moments with them, and I'll never forget it."

"And then," the man cuts back in, his baritone drawl replacing the girl's shy, sweet delivery, *"Subject Zero woke up, still a girl, still a lifetime to live."*

"Emma! You didn't let me go! You just didn't call!" Cassie shouts into the radio, forgetting its fragility. "Emma! I'm here!"

A radio jingle chimes in, not unlike the vasectomy promo spot only with more production value.

"The Gate is changing the world and how we live in it," the man carries on.

"Please!" Cassie cries into the alarm clock, as though the speakers are receivers, as though Emma is on the other end, listening. She knows it's her. She knows she, Cassie, is the one who was let go.

"Book your appointment today. Just call—"

Cassie throws the alarm clock onto the ground and it shatters into particles of plastic and wires and silence.

CASSIE ORDERS A PEPPERMINT TEA and sits down at a table by the window at the back of the coffee shop. Their table. Hers and Emma's. The barista knew her order; Cassie comes here too much. She comes here too much like the others that come here, and will stay here like the others that stay here, ordering a hot drink out of necessity, occupying a table for hours; tables here are garnished with MacBooks and coffee rings and empty ceramic cups with lipstick stains. Tables here are garnished with something she hasn't noticed before.

More than half the people in the coffee shop have their eyes closed with four white circular stickers affixed to their skin; one on each temple, and one on either side of their forehead. These stickers are connected to thin white wires, like EKG leads, that connect to phones or laptops. There is a person beside Cassie, one table over, that is in the same trance as the others. She leans over until she can see the person's cellphone screen. There is an application open that reads:

THE GATE

PROGRAM: VIATOR

ELAPSED TIME: 0:02:53.21

VIRTUAL TIME: 29 YRS, 9 MTHS, 13 DAYS

Below this, to the bottom right of the screen, is an advertisement for a funeral home, a tiny box that you can click with the touch of a finger.

Cassie looks away from the phone and studies the man. He's wearing a pair of blue jeans, a white V-neck T-shirt that looks two sizes too big, and a black toque struggling to hide his hair loss. Cheekbones protrude through his skin like knives. He is a skeleton dressed in skin dressed in clothes, layered like a matryoshka doll, and it is clear to Cassie that at the middle of it all, once all the shells have been removed, there is a football-sized tumour somewhere inside his body. He is soggy from chemo. He is inches from death. He is living three decades longer than he has any business to live, right here in the coffee shop, a half-full coffee in front of him still hot, still steam rising from it, steam billowing into the air, dancing to music that nobody else can hear. Five seconds later he gasps, opens his eyes, looks around like he doesn't know where he is, or when, or who.

Cassie stands up and canvasses the coffee shop, stops at every person with their eyes closed, every person with thin white wires running from a device, from a laptop or a phone, to little round stickers affixed to their foreheads and temples. She looks at their screens. They are all the same. They are all connected to The Gate. Some for a few seconds, some for a few minutes, which means that some have been living in The Gate for months, or years, or decades. All while sitting at their tables with still-hot beverages, here but not really, there but not really. The program names change from person to person. VIATOR is a popular one. EFFUGIUM. OBSEQUIUM. CURSUS. AMARE.

There's a mother and a son sitting at a table at the opposite end of the shop, whisper-shouting, and Cassie realizes in that moment how quiet it is. Everybody else sits at their seats, and whether they are hooked into The Gate or not, they are all, still, in their own world. They are all, still, attached to devices and their cobweb wires. The son is wearing ripped blue jeans, a black Radiohead T-shirt, black Cons, and his hair looks like Eddie Vedder's mid-'90s. The mother is a lady, and that is the only way Cassie can describe her: straight-backed, so straight-backed, even as she argues with her boy. Hands crossed on her lap, leg crossed on her chair. Not a hair out of place.

"I don't want to do it!"

"This isn't a choice, Braxton," the mother shout-whispers through a fake plastic smile, her eyes darting back and forth, surveying the coffee shop, without moving her head a fraction in either direction. "It'll be five minutes at most."

"Fifty years, I'm not an idiot! I know what this thing does too!"

She slides her hands across the table, handing the boy the white round stickers and thin wires. "Put them on, now."

"Mom ..." The boy's tone changes.

"Can I help you?" the mother asks Cassie.

She's come right up to the table without noticing. She looks at the boy, at the mother.

"Sorry."

Cassie walks back to her and Emma's table and sits down, but keeps watching the boy and his mother until the boy relents. Places the stickers on his temples and forehead. Relents like a child does when finally agreeing to do a chore: taking out the garbage, loading the dishwasher, raking the leaves. His head drops, shoulders slump, and he manages a defiant eye-roll before the mother presses her finger against the cool glass surface of an iPad. Such a simple gesture, so politely done, and then the boy closes his eyes gently, as though rocked to sleep by the lullaby of drink orders.

Cassie watches the boy, and only the boy, as he sits across from his expectant mother, hands resting against the table along with a colourful drink she bought him (pink lemonade, Cassie thinks), a black Americano she sips on with wide eyes, and an iPad counting down from five minutes. Fifty years. Same. Underneath the boy's eyelids, Cassie sees his eyes sprinting from side to side, REM on double espresso.

Why.

Cassie is staring. She's come right up to the table, again without noticing. Without leaving her own table. The mother notices. She gets up, walks across the coffee shop, stops at Cassie and Emma's table. Stands until Cassie notices her.

"It's impolite to stare."

"Sorry."

Cassie looks away from the boy, to the mother.

"You don't agree?"

"No." She looks at the boy.

There are three minutes left.

"I don't agree."

"He needed to change."

"He wanted to change?"

"I needed him to change."

"No," Cassie says, "I don't agree."

"Well, I can't say that it's any of your business."

The mother turns away. Her high heels tap a rhythm as she returns to her table. Nobody is dancing.

When five minutes are up, the length of a song, the length of a lullaby, the mother reaches forward and pulls the white round stickers from the boy's face. His eyes flutter open. He looks around, looks lost until he meets eyes with his mother.

"Braxton?" The mother's tone changes.

The boy smiles a plastic smile. Sips his still-cold pink lemonade. His mother breaks down in tears of joy.

Cassie can hear Emma's voice. *"I met someone and let them go, but with help from The Gate ..."*

You did what? Cassie thinks. *What did you do? How many years did you spend with me, and without me?*

Emma won't come here.

Cassie leaves her table, their table, leaves her peppermint tea, subtle pink lipstick stains populating the ceramic rim.

Still hot.

THE GATE'S HEADQUARTERS are in a brownstone building in the belly of the Exchange District. There is an old woman sitting at a bus stop a few houses down, a walker at her side, stickers on her temples and forehead, wires running from her head into her purse, a delicate light emanating from within it. Her eyes are closed, she is dead to the world, smiling blankly, early for the bus and killing time. Cassie wonders if, when her journey is over, she will remember what bus she is waiting for, or that she is waiting at all?

A bell tinkles when Cassie opens the door to the brownstone building, a heavy door painted a deep red that she strained to move, and she thinks, as she enters the reception area, how odd it is to have such a small bell for such a large door. The reception area is a bombardment of white, a blizzard broken only by hardwood flooring (a white shag area rug over the floor) and cardboard moving boxes stacked neatly beside a glass reception desk. A young man dressed in a white shirt, white khaki pants, and flip-flops greets her, smiling as though he has put on the expression like his clothing.

"Welcome to The Gate," the young man says. "Please, excuse the mess. We're currently in the process of moving to serve you better."

There is no mess.

"Hey." Cassie approaches the young man, who maintains eye contact with her unblinkingly. "I'm looking for somebody and I thought you could help."

"Certainly," the young man says.

"Her name's Emma. She took this ... program. She used this thing."

"Sorry," the young man smiles apologetically, the same smile, "I can't help you."

"But you said ..."

"Two things. One, there is an abundance of Emmas," the young man says, "and two, we can't give out personal information on anybody who has purchased our application."

"She was on the radio," Cassie says, "I heard her on the radio. There's only one Emma. Subject Zero. That's what you called her."

"We can't give out personal information on anybody who has purchased our application."

"You said that."

"Can I help you with anything else?"

Cassie stares at the young man intently, then scans the room. White bookshelves, empty; white plastic chairs surrounding a circular glass coffee table, empty; a white door behind the young man with a small window at its centre revealing a white hallway with more white doors haloed by white fluorescent light fixtures protruding from a white-tiled ceiling, layered just like that. She looks at the young man again. He will pack his smile into the cardboard boxes along with the other furnishings.

"No," Cassie says. "You can't."

Cassie pulls the door open with great effort, the bell tinkles to announce her departure, and she steps outside. The old woman is still waiting for the bus, smiling blankly, eyes closed, open someplace else.

"Tansi," Cassie whispers to the old woman, but then touches her lips.

How do I know that? she thinks. *How do I know to say that?*

Cassie sits beside her. She imagines the hard green bus bench to be the edge of a hospital bed. She imagines the sunlight to be filtered through the thin window, and resting solely on the woman's face. On Emma's face. The woman's hands are crossed politely over her lap. Cassie puts her hand over the woman's and squeezes gently. She can feel the woman's tiny bones. She can feel the woman's loose skin stiffened in the chill. Another hand. More warmth. The woman's eyelids are shivering, like her hands and brittle fingers. The woman is dreaming. How many times did Cassie sit at Emma's side, in all the dreams that she has had? How long has the old woman been sitting here, waiting? How long has she been so cold?

"I'll wait with you," she says, and does, and her hands don't move from the woman's.

Minutes later, years later, a bus appears on the horizon. The old woman will miss the bus. Cassie moves to wake her, to pull the cobwebs away, but a hand touches her arm to stop her.

"That won't end well," a young woman says. She's a tiny woman with dyed purple hair in a pixie cut, thick-rimmed black glasses, an iskwē T-shirt, skinny jeans, and Toms.

"Why?"

The young woman sits down beside Cassie. "She'll be lost."

"Lost?"

"Just watch a moment," the young woman says and nods in the old woman's direction while Cassie watches. The bus is two stops away, roaring like a distant storm. An alarm goes off from inside the old woman's purse. Slow rise ring tone. A song that keeps playing, its metronome beat, its hypnotic chime. It plays until the old woman's eyelids open like butterfly wings. She looks around, looks at every-thing, looks at Cassie, and then smiles, really smiles.

Cassie moves her hands away from the old woman's.

The old woman reaches into her purse, pulls out her phone, and turns off the ring tone. The screen displays what Cassie saw on so many devices at the coffee shop: AETERNUM.

The bus is one stop away. The old woman rises to her feet, pulls the walker in front of her body, and welcomes the bus at her stop just in time. The bus jerks into movement, lowers flat against the curb so that the old woman can get on easily, then pulls away into traffic.

"The end stage of any program within The Gate is reorientation," the young woman says. "Layperson's terms? That lady was gone for one hundred and fifty years. The reorientation means that she gets reminded of where she was, and what she was doing, right before she hooked in. Got it?"

"You work for The Gate?"

"Dude," the young woman says, "I *designed* The Gate." She extends her hand, and Cassie shakes it. "I'm Pyper."

"Cassie."

"Yeah, I know who you are."

"You what?"

"That's why I came out here, Cassie. I saw you in the lobby, CCTV style, and, I don't know, I just had to come out and see you. It's like watching a movie you've seen a million times and running into the star."

"I don't understand."

"Of course, of course, of course," Pyper says like a record skipping, shaking her head like she, too, is on repeat. "Sorry." She breathes in, and out, methodically. "You're here for Emma."

"Yeah." Cassie feels her heart skip. "You know her?"

"Well, I'd say I know you more than her, but I know her too."

"Subject Zero."

"Subject Zero." Pyper spreads her hands out in front of her like she's smoothing a bedsheet. "She was on my table, Cassie. I hooked her in. First civilian. For her, it was all about, you know, teaching her what she'd missed out on when she didn't call you."

"Teaching her," Cassie repeats. "Like a lesson?"

"That's what we're always trying to do, in some way, shape, or form," Pyper says. "Take that old lady, Clementine." She nods into traffic as though Clementine is still right there. "She wanted to delay death, which she did, but we wanted her to enjoy and appreciate life. Two birds, one stone."

"AETERNUM? What does that mean?"

"Oh," Pyper chuckles dismissively, "that's ... we just want to give these programs cool names. That mean something, too, of course. That's Latin, they're mostly all Latin: Latin sounds cool, good for cool names. AETERNUM means forever."

"You wanted to teach Emma about what she'd missed out on," Cassie states, "but she never called me. You didn't teach her anything."

Pyper puts a hand on Cassie's shoulder. "It doesn't always work."

"I was here to find her," Cassie says, staring out into traffic, saying these words to nobody but herself.

"I know you were."

They don't talk for what seems like forever. They both stare out into traffic, their silence serenaded by car horns. Pyper sighs.

"I shouldn't tell you this, but because I'm telling you that I shouldn't tell you this, I'm clearly going to tell you this."

"Tell me." Cassie turns toward Pyper desperately.

"She was here today, like, just before you got here."

"What?"

"Cassie." Pyper pauses, and then continues. "She came here to forget you."

"Forget me? Why? How?"

"It's a new program. It's a long journey, without the reorientation. Only, this time, it's not just the place they aren't reminded of, but the people. A person. That's the best way I can describe it."

"How long is the journey? How long does it take to forget somebody?"

"It depends on the person they're trying to forget. The Gate, it's intuitive."

"I couldn't forget about Emma. I dream about Emma."

"Yeah, you could." Pyper stands up. "People can go a week without water. We'd never make a program that lasted that long. But a day? Yeah. People sign waivers anyway, just in case."

"A day?" Cassie tries to do the math, and then tries to forget the math. "A day isn't that long."

"Every minute is ten years, about. An hour is six hundred years. A day is ..."

"Fourteen thousand—"

"—and four hundred years," Pyper says.

"How long has she been gone for? When did she leave here?"

"She just left," Pyper says. "She just left right before you got here."

"I have to ..." Cassie looks around frantically.

"Here." Pyper extends her hand. Cassie takes her hand and is slipped a folded yellow Post-it Note. "I'm not sure you were dreaming."

"I'm not sure I was dreaming."

Pyper nods. "It was really good to meet you."

"What's it called?"

"What's what called?"

"The program she got to forget me. What's it called? What does it mean?" Latin. Cool language. Cool names. Latin to English.

"Eloise," Pyper says. "It means Eloise." She smiles, then walks away hurriedly toward the brownstone building. Pushes the red door open, disappears inside.

Cassie looks down at her hand, palming the folded yellow paper. She unfolds it delicately to find an address written on it in black Sharpie.

EMMA LIVES IN A TWO-STOREY HOUSE, cookie cutter, indistinguishable from the next, and so on et cetera: an upper-class neighbourhood, a neighbourhood of mirrors. Cassie stops on the boulevard. She looks to the left, then looks to the right, and sees the same thing either way: a row of white teeth and picket fence braces. Manufactured perfection. It's been seventeen minutes since she left the bus stop. It's been one hundred and seventy years since she left the bus stop. Each red light, she counted the seconds as though they were years. The car ride took forever. AETERNUM.

"Can I help you?"

A woman answers the door. Cassie instantly recognizes her as Emma's mother. She is how Emma will look two decades from now. Two minutes from now.

"Is Emma home?"

"Yes," Emma's mother says. She looks behind her, into the house, and then back at Cassie. "She's not feeling well, though. Said she was going to sleep it off."

"Oh." Cassie checks the time. Counts the seconds. "Can I just see her?"

"Can it wait until tomorrow? She'll feel better then."

"No, it can't wait until then."

"I'm sorry, but ..." Emma's mother stops, and looks at Cassie carefully. Her eyes widen. "You're Cassie."

Cassie nods. "She's talked about me?"

"You are on her every breath," Emma's mother says as though reciting lyrics to a song.

"We only met once," Cassie says, but she is agreeing with Emma's mother, not arguing with her.

She pictures their first meeting and it feels like a remembered dream, sitting by the window at the back of the coffee shop, Cassie with her peppermint tea, Emma with her decaf Americano. Cassie had asked her, soon after she'd sat down with her, why she bothered getting a decaf. Didn't that defeat the entire purpose of coffee? Emma, without hesitating, with a devilish grin, had responded that her heart was already beating too fast. She used frat boy pickup lines without apology. She didn't look at you, she looked into you, and Cassie couldn't look at her for too long. It was like staring at the sun.

"She called you?"

"She called me."

"She stared at your number, as much as she stared at your picture."

"I never had a picture."

"Come in."

"Ekosani." Cassie walks inside and takes off her shoes.

"You know Cree?"

Cassie can hear the word off the mother's lips. The mother. Nicole. She can hear the words off Nicole's lips. She can see Nicole's hands, cupped like so, pulling smoke toward her hair, her eyes, her mouth, her heart. She can see her feather smoke toward Cassie, and Cassie repeating the same motion, Cassie repeating the same word, Cassie repeating the same word to Emma, Emma lying in her hospital bed for so many years, so many minutes. Ekosani. She can see this all in her dream. She can see this all in her memory.

"A little bit," she says.

EMMA IS LYING ON HER BED, her hands crossed over her chest, four white round stickers affixed to her temples and forehead, a thin wire snaking its way to an iPhone resting at her hip. She is wearing grey sweats, a navy shirt, and has bare feet. Her eyes are closed, eyelids shivering with dreams. The curtains are shut and the room is lit by the glow of her phone, painting everything in a soft white light. Cassie sits beside her on the bed, looks at Emma, and thinks of how perfectly she looks just how she, Cassie, remembers her. She takes Emma's hand then slowly, reluctantly, looks down at the cellphone screen.

THE GATE

PROGRAM: ELOISE

ELAPSED TIME: 42:33.08

VIRTUAL TIME: 425 YRS, 9 MTHS, 8 DAYS

"Why did you do that?" Cassie whispers into Emma's ear, the closest she's ever been to Emma, closer than when they met, when they just collapsed into each other across the rounded table, but never touched. She picks up the iPhone. There is a small red circle at the bottom of the screen, centred under the virtual time Emma has been gone. EXITUS. Exit. There is no reorientation. She is not supposed to remember. She is not supposed to remember Cassie. Cassie touches her fingertip against the red circle as though the glass might shatter, and she with it.

Moments later, seconds later, just seconds, Emma's eyelids flutter open. She's facing the window and stares at a shaft of light stretching across the room from a crack in the curtain. She stares at it for a long time, then looks away from it, scans the room, from right to left, until resting her eyes on Cassie.

"Tansi." Cassie squeezes her hand and smiles.

Emma props herself up onto her elbows, and in the process lets go of Cassie's hand. Her eyes do another lap of the room and she looks at Cassie again, curiously. Brow furrowed. Head tilted. "Where am I?"

"You're in your bedroom."

"I don't know this place."

Cassie doesn't say anything.

"Who are you?"

Cassie fights back tears, tells Emma her name, and waits. There is a shaft of light between them. They are both staring at it.

"I don't know you."

Cassie lets all the air out of her lungs before breathing again. Was four hundred years so much easier than a phone call? Was it easier to forget? Emma's forgotten everything just to forget her. Cassie reaches forward, and when her hand is close to Emma's face, Emma closes her eyes. Cassie pulls the thin white wires out of the stickers, one by one, and then peels the stickers away from Emma's temples and forehead, each time brushing her fingertips against her skin, brushing her fingertips across the tiny follicles of hair, like she's reading braille, like there's a story written there that only she can read.

"That's okay."

"What's okay?"

Cassie leans forward, Emma's eyes still closed, collapses toward Emma, feels the shaft of light warm against her cheek, and then touches her lips against Emma's, just for a moment, just for a few seconds, just for forever. Then, Cassie moves away, moves off the bed, walks toward Emma's bedroom door.

She wants to say goodbye, but there's no word for goodbye in Cree. She knows that. She was taught that. Remembers it clearly now. Remembers all of it. She stands facing the door. It's a white door. There are white walls. There is a desk to the right and a wastepaper basket between the door frame and the desk. There is one crumpled-up piece of paper in the basket. Cassie bends down, picks it up, then straightens. Facing the door, then facing her hand, palming the crumpled-up paper. She unfolds it delicately to find her school picture, and on the back of it, her phone number in pencil, smudged almost enough to be illegible, more like trees within a dead forest in the distance.

Cassie thumbs the smeared numbers. "You silly girl," she says, and reaches for the door handle.

"What did you say?" Emma asks.

Cassie turns around to find Emma standing beside her bed, eyes open, eyes fixed on her. Emma touches her lips, runs her fingertips across them.

Cassie thinks of what to say. Searches for the words, like they are dancing in the air within the shaft of light, dancing to music that only she can hear. And Emma.

She pockets the cut-out wallet photograph.

"Do you want to go for coffee?" Cassie asks.

"Ehe."

"Americano, right? Decaf."

"Right," she says, then smiles. "My heart's already beating too fast."

FINIS

ABOUT THE
CONTRIBUTORS

NATHAN ADLER is the author of *Wrist* (Kegedonce Press) and editor of *Bawaajigan: Stories of Power* (Exile Editions). He has an MFA in creative writing from UBC, is a first-place winner of the Indigenous Arts & Stories Challenge, and is a recipient of a Hnatyshyn REVEAL Indigenous Art Award for Literature. He is Anishinaabe and Jewish, and a member of Lac des Mille Lacs First Nation.

GABRIEL CASTILLOUX CALDERON (they/them) is nij-manidowag (Two-Spirit) Mi'kmaq, Algonquin, Scottish, and French Canadian. They currently thrive in Treaty 6 territory's Amiskwacîwâskahikan (Edmonton). Gabe is actively involved in their Indigenous culture and ceremonies, and proudly celebrates a drug- and alcohol-free life. Gabe has won several short story awards, and they are a member of Breath in Poetry, the second-place champions of the 2019 Canadian Festival of Spoken Word team slam poetry competition. Gabe has also been chosen to represent the Two-Spirit community as Mr. Two Spirit International 2019–20.

ADAM GARNET JONES (Cree/Métis/Danish) is a Two-Spirit screen-writer, director, beadworker, and novelist from Amiskwacîwâskahikan (Edmonton). Adam came into his own as a filmmaker with the release of his first feature, *Fire Song*, at the Toronto International Film Festival in 2015. *Fire Song* went on to win the Audience Choice Award at imagineNATIVE before picking up three more audience choice awards and two jury prizes for best film at other festivals. Before going into production, the script for *Fire Song* won the Writers Guild of Canada's Jim Burt Screenwriting Prize. Adam is now focusing on writing fiction and creating custom beadwork, primarily for Indigenous artists. His first novel, *Fire Song* (based on the film), was published in spring 2018. *Publishers Weekly* called it "striking and remarkable," and the *Globe and Mail* said, "*Fire Song* is unquestionably necessary ... because of its subject matter, perspective and voice." The book received a starred review from *Kirkus* and was named an honour book by CODE's Burt Award for First Nations, Inuit and Métis Young Adult Literature. It also won a bronze medal for young adult fiction from the Independent Publisher Book Awards. *Fire Song* has topped innumerable "best of" lists of the year's LGBT YA literature in the United States and Canada. Adam works to support Indigenous filmmakers at Telefilm Canada as content analyst and Indigenous liaison.

MARI KURISATO is the pen name for a disabled, LGBTQIA, tribally enrolled Cote First Nation Ojibwe woman who lives in Denver, Colorado, with her wife and son. She has written two self-published books, and her short fiction has appeared in the anthologies *Things We Are Not: M-Brane SF Presents New Tales of the Queer* and *Absolute Power: Tales of Queer Villainy!* (Northwest Press). She is hard at work on her next novel, seeking an agent, and spending too much time on Twitter and in MMOs. Find her on Twitter at @CyborgN8VMari and online at polychromantium.com.

DARCIE LITTLE BADGER is a Lipan Apache writer with a PhD in ocean-ography. Her debut novel, *Elatsoe*, was published by Levine Querido in August 2020 and is a BookExpo 2020 Young Adult Buzz Finalist. Darcie co-wrote *Strangelands*, a comic series in the Humanoids' H1 universe. Her short fiction, non-fiction, and comics have appeared in multiple publications, including *Nightmare Magazine*, *Strange Horizons*, and *The Dark*, and were featured in an episode on the pod-cast *LeVar Burton Reads*. She lives on both coasts of the United States and is engaged to a veterinarian who cosplays as Cassandra Pentaghast and Luke Skywalker.

KAI MINOSH PYLE is a Two-Spirit Métis and Baawiting Nishnaabe writer originally from Green Bay, Wisconsin, living in Bde Ota Otunwe (Minneapolis, Minnesota). They have been published in both creative and scholarly journals such as *PRISM international*, *Transgender Studies Quarterly*, *Cloudthroat*, and *The Activist History Review*. Their current projects include editing a zine of Two-Spirit writing, pursuing a PhD on Two-Spirit Anishinaabe history, and, as always, learning their ancestral languages.

DAVID A. ROBERTSON is the winner of the Governor General's Literary Award, the Beatrice Mosionier Indigenous Writer of the Year Award, and the John Hirsch Award for Most Promising Manitoba Writer. His books include *When We Were Alone* (winner of the Governor General's Award, a finalist for the TD Canadian Children's Literature Award, and a McNally Robinson Best Book for Young People); *Will I See?* (winner of the Manuela Dias Book Design and Illustration Award, Graphic Novel category); the YA novel *Strangers* (recipient of the Michael Van Rooy Award for Genre Fiction); and *Monsters* (a McNally Robinson Best Book for Young People). Through his writings about Canada's Indigenous peoples, David educates as well as entertains, reflecting Indigenous cultures, histories, and communities while illuminating many contemporary issues. David is a member of Norway House Cree Nation. He lives in Winnipeg.

JAYE SIMPSON is an Oji-Cree Saulteaux Indigiqueer whose roots hail from the Sapotaweyak, Keeseekoose, and Skownan Cree Nations. they are published in several magazines including *Poetry Is Dead*, *This Magazine*, *PRISM international*, *SAD Mag*, *GUTS*, *subTerrain*,

Grain, and *Room*. they are in two Arsenal Pulp Press anthologies: *Hustling Verse* (2019) and *Love after the End* (2020). *it was never going to be okay* (Nightwood Editions) is their first book of poetry. they are a displaced Indigenous person resisting, ruminating, and residing on xʷməθkʷəy̓əm (Musqueam), səĺilwəta?ɬ (Tsleil-Waututh), and sḵwx̱wú7mesh (Squamish) First Nations territories.

NAZBAH TOM, Diné, is a somatic practitioner. They support individuals and groups through a process of embodied transformation using a combination of conversation, breath work, new skills, bodywork, and gestures. Their work aims to humanize and reconnect us to ourselves, each other, and our land. In between working with individuals and groups, they do their best to capture poems and short stories haunting them at all hours of the day.

JOSHUA WHITEHEAD is an Oji-Cree/nêhiyâw, Two-Spirit/Indigiqueer member of Peguis First Nation (Treaty 1). He is the author of the poetry collection *full-metal indigiqueer* (Talonbooks, 2017) and the novel *Jonny Appleseed* (Arsenal Pulp Press, 2018), which was longlisted for the Scotiabank Giller Prize; shortlisted for the Governor General's Award for Fiction, the Amazon First Novel Award, the Carol Shields Winnipeg Book Award, the Firecracker Award, and the Indigenous Voices Award; and won a Lambda Literary Award for Gay Fiction and the Georges Bugnet Award for Fiction. He is the winner of the Governor General's History Award for the Indigenous Arts & Stories Challenge in 2016. He is working on a PhD in Indigenous Literatures and Cultures in the University of Calgary's English department (Treaty 7).

joshuawhitehead.ca